FAMILY
HAPPINESS

FAMILY HAPPINESS

Stories

LEO TOLSTOY

HARPER**PERENNIAL** CLASSIC**STORIES**

NEW YORK • LONDON • TORONTO • SYDNEY • NEW DELHI • AUCKLAND

FIRST HARPER PERENNIAL CLASSIC STORIES EDITION PUBLISHED 2009.

Designed by Justin Dodd

Library of Congress Cataloging-in-Publication Data is available upon request.

ISBN 978-0-06-177373-0

09 10 11 12 13   OV/RRD   10 9 8 7 6 5 4 3 2 1

CONTENTS

FAMILY
HAPPINESS

FAMILY HAPPINESS

[1859]

Part I

I

We were in mourning for my mother, who had died in the autumn, and I spent all that winter alone in the country with Kátya and Sónya.

Kátya was an old friend of the family, our governess who had brought us all up, and I had known and loved her since my earliest recollections. Sónya was my younger sister. It was a dark and sad winter which we spent in our old house of Pokróvskoe. The weather was cold and so windy that the snowdrifts came higher than the windows; the panes were almost always dimmed by frost, and we seldom walked or drove anywhere throughout the winter. Our visitors were few, and those who came brought no addition of cheerfulness or happiness to the household. They all wore sad faces and spoke low, as if they were afraid of waking someone; they never laughed, but sighed and often shed tears as they looked at me and especially at little Sónya in her black frock. The feeling of death clung to the house; the air was still filled with the grief and horror of death. My mother's room was kept locked; and whenever I passed it on my way to bed, I felt a strange uncomfortable impulse to look into that cold empty room.

I was then seventeen; and in the very year of her death my mother was intending to move to Petersburg, in order to take me into society. The loss of my mother was a great grief to me; but I must confess to another feeling behind that grief—a feeling that though I was young and pretty (so everybody told me), I was wasting a second winter in the solitude of the country. Before the winter ended, this sense of dejection, solitude, and simple boredom increased to such an extent that I refused to leave my room or open the piano or take up a book. When Kátya urged me to find some occupation, I said that I did not feel able for it; but in my heart I said, 'What is the good of it? What is the good of doing anything, when the best part of my life is being wasted like this?' And to this question, tears were my only answer.

I was told that I was growing thin and losing my looks; but even this failed to interest me. What did it matter? For whom? I felt that my whole life was bound to go on in the same solitude and helpless dreariness, from which I had myself no strength and even no wish to escape. Towards the end of winter Kátya became anxious about me and determined to make an effort to take me abroad. But money was needed for this, and we hardly knew how our affairs stood after my mother's death. Our guardian, who was to come and clear up our position, was expected every day.

In March he arrived.

'Well, thank God!' Kátya said to me one day, when I was walking up and down the room like a shadow, without occupation, without a thought, and without a wish. 'Sergéy Mikháylych has arrived; he has sent to inquire about us and means to come here for dinner. You must rouse yourself, dear Máshechka,' she added, 'or what will he think of you? He was so fond of you all.'

Sergéy Mikháylych was our near neighbour, and, though a much younger man, had been a friend of my father's. His coming was likely to change our plans and to make it possible to leave the country; and also I had grown up in the habit of love and regard for him; and when Kátya begged me to rouse myself, she guessed rightly that it would give me especial pain to show to disadvantage before him, more than before any other of our friends. Like everyone in the house, from Kátya and his god-daughter Sónya down to the helper in the stables, I loved him from old habit; and also he had a special significance for me, owing to a remark which my mother had once made in my presence. 'I should like you to marry a man like him,' she said. At the time this seemed to me strange and even unpleasant. My ideal husband was quite different: he was to be thin, pale, and sad; and Sergéy Mikháylych was middle-aged, tall, robust, and always, as it seemed to me, in good spirits. But still my mother's words stuck in my head; and even six years before this time, when I was eleven, and he still said 'thou' to me, and played with me, and called me by the pet-name of 'violet'—even then I sometimes asked myself in a fright, 'What *shall* I do, if he suddenly wants to marry me?'

Before our dinner, to which Kátya made an addition of sweets and a dish of spinach, Sergéy Mikháylych arrived. From the window I watched him drive up to the house in a small sleigh; but as soon as it turned the corner, I hastened to the drawing-room, meaning to pretend that his visit was a complete surprise. But when I heard his tramp and loud voice and Kátya's footsteps in the hall, I lost patience and went to meet him myself. He was holding Kátya's hand, talking loud, and smiling. When he saw me, he stopped and looked at me for a time without bowing. I was uncomfortable and felt myself blushing.

'Can this be really you?' he said in his plain decisive way, walking towards me with his arms apart. 'Is so great a change possible? How grown-up you are! I used to call you "violet", but now you are a rose in full bloom!'

He took my hand in his own large hand and pressed it so hard that it almost hurt. Expecting him to kiss my hand, I bent towards him, but he only pressed it again and looked straight into my eyes with the old firmness and cheerfulness in his face.

It was six years since I had seen him last. He was much changed—older and darker in complexion; and he now wore whiskers which did not become him at all; but much remained the same—his simple manner, the large features of his honest open face, his bright intelligent eyes, his friendly, almost boyish, smile.

Five minutes later he had ceased to be a visitor and had become the friend of us all, even of the servants, whose visible eagerness to wait on him proved their pleasure at his arrival.

He behaved quite unlike the neighbours who had visited us after my mother's death. They had thought it necessary to be silent when they sat with us, and to shed tears. He, on the contrary, was cheerful and talkative, and said not a word about my mother, so that this indifference seemed strange to me at first and even improper on the part of so close a friend. But I understood later that what seemed indifference was sincerity, and I felt grateful for it. In the evening Kátya poured out tea, sitting in her old place in the drawing-room, where she used to sit in my mother's lifetime; Sónya and I sat near him; our old butler Grigóri had hunted out one of my father's pipes and brought it to him; and he began to walk up and down the room as he used to do in past days.

'How many terrible changes there are in this house, when one thinks of it all!' he said, stopping in his walk.

'Yes,' said Kátya with a sigh; and then she put the lid on the samovar and looked at him, quite ready to burst out crying.

'I suppose you remember your father?' he said, turning to me.

'Not clearly,' I answered.

'How happy you would have been together now!' he added in a low voice, looking thoughtfully at my face above the eyes. 'I was very fond of him,' he added in a still lower tone, and it seemed to me that his eyes were shining more than usual.

'And now God has taken her too!' said Kátya; and at once she laid her napkin on the teapot, took out her handkerchief, and began to cry.

'Yes, the changes in this house are terrible,' he repeated, turning away. 'Sónya, show me your toys,' he added after a little and went off to the parlour. When he had gone, I looked at Kátya with eyes full of tears.

'What a splendid friend he is!' she said. And, though he was no relation, I did really feel a kind of warmth and comfort in the sympathy of this good man.

I could hear him moving about in the parlour with Sónya, and the sound of her high childish voice. I sent tea to him there; and I heard him sit down at the piano and strike the keys with Sónya's little hands.

Then his voice came—'Márya Alexándrovna, come here and play something.'

I liked his easy behaviour to me and his friendly tone of command; I got up and went to him.

'Play this,' he said, opening a book of Beethoven's music at the *adagio* of the 'Moonlight Sonata.' 'Let me hear how you play,' he added, and went off to a corner of the room, carrying his cup with him.

I somehow felt that with him it was impossible to refuse or to say beforehand that I played badly: I sat down obediently at the piano and began to play as well as I could; yet I was afraid of criticism, because I knew that he understood and enjoyed music. The *adagio* suited the remembrance of past days evoked by our conversation at tea, and I believe that I played it fairly well. But he would not let me play the *scherzo.* 'No,' he said, coming up to me; 'you don't play that right; don't go on; but the first movement was not bad; you seem to be musical.' This moderate praise pleased me so much that I even reddened. I felt it pleasant and strange that a friend of my father's, and his contemporary, should no longer treat me like a child but speak to me seriously. Kátya now went upstairs to put Sónya to bed, and we were left alone in the parlour.

He talked to me about my father, and about the beginning of their friendship and the happy days they had spent together, while I was still busy with lesson-books and toys; and his talk put my father before me in quite a new light, as a man of simple and delightful character. He asked me too about my tastes, what I read and what I intended to do, and gave me advice. The man of mirth and jest who used to tease me and make me toys had disappeared, here was a serious, simple, and affectionate friend, for whom I could not help feeling respect and sympathy. It was easy and pleasant to talk to him; and yet I felt an involuntary strain also. I was anxious about each word I spoke: I wished so much to earn for my own sake the love which had been given me already merely because I was my father's daughter.

After putting Sónya to bed, Kátya joined us and began to complain to him of my apathy, about which I had said nothing.

'So she never told me the most important thing of all!' he said, smiling and shaking his head reproachfully at me.

'Why tell you?' I said. 'It is very tiresome to talk about, and it will pass off.' (I really felt now, not only that my dejection would pass off, but that it had already passed off, or rather had never existed.)

'It is a bad thing,' he said, 'not to be able to stand solitude. Can it be that you are a young lady?'

'Of course, I am a young lady,' I answered, laughing.

'Well, I can't praise a young lady who is alive only when people are admiring her, but as soon as she is left alone, collapses and finds nothing to her taste—one who is all for show and has no resources in herself.'

'You have a flattering opinion of me!' I said, just for the sake of saying something.

He was silent for a little. Then he said: 'Yes; your likeness to your father means something. There is something in you . . . ,' and his kind attentive look again flattered me and made me feel a pleasant embarrassment.

I noticed now for the first time that his face, which gave one at first the impression of high spirits, had also an expression peculiar to himself—bright at first and then more and more attentive and rather sad.

'You ought not to be bored and you cannot be,' he said; 'you have music, which you appreciate, books, study; your whole life lies before you, and now or never is the time to prepare for it and save yourself future regrets. A year hence it will be too late.'

He spoke to me like a father or an uncle, and I felt that he kept a constant check upon himself, in order to keep on my level. Though I was hurt that he considered me as inferior to himself, I was pleased that for me alone he thought it necessary to try to be different.

For the rest of the evening he talked about business with Kátya.

'Well, good-bye, dear friends,' he said. Then he got up, came towards me, and took my hand.

'When shall we see you again?' asked Kátya.

'In spring,' he answered, still holding my hand. 'I shall go now to Danílovka' (this was another property of ours), 'look into things there and make what arrangements I can; then I go to Moscow on business of my own; and in summer we shall meet again.'

'Must you really be away so long?' I asked, and I felt terribly grieved. I had really hoped to see him every day, and I felt a sudden shock of regret, and a fear that my depression would return. And my face and voice must have made this plain.

'You must find more to do and not get depressed,' he said; and I thought his tone too cool and unconcerned. 'I shall put you through an examination in spring,' he added, letting go my hand and not looking at me.

When we saw him off in the hall, he put on his fur coat in a hurry and still avoided looking at me. 'He is taking a deal of trouble for nothing!' I thought 'Does he think me so anxious that he should look at me? He is a good man, a very good man; but that's all.'

That evening, however, Kátya and I sat up late, talking, not about him but about our plans for the summer, and where we should spend next winter and what we should do then. I had ceased to ask that terrible question—what is the good of it all? Now it seemed quite plain and simple: the proper object of life was happiness, and I promised myself much happiness ahead. It seemed as if our gloomy old house had suddenly become full of light and life.

II

Meanwhile spring arrived. My old dejection passed away and gave place to the unrest which spring brings with it, full of dreams and vague hopes and desires. Instead of living as I had done at the beginning of winter, I read and played the piano and gave lessons to Sónya; but also I often went into the garden and wandered for long alone through the avenues, or sat on a bench there; and Heaven knows what my thoughts and wishes and hopes were at such times. Sometimes at night, especially if there was a moon, I sat by my bedroom window till dawn; sometimes, when Kátya was not watching, I stole out into the garden wearing only a wrapper and ran through the dew as far as the pond; and once I went all the way to the open fields and walked right round the garden alone at night.

I find it difficult now to recall and understand the dreams which then filled my imagination. Even when I *can* recall them, I find it hard to believe that my dreams were just like that: they were so strange and so remote from life.

Sergéy Mikháylych kept his promise: he returned from his travels at the end of May.

His first visit to us was in the evening and was quite unexpected. We were sitting in the veranda, preparing for tea. By this time the garden was all green, and the nightingales had taken up their quarters for the whole of St. Peter's Fast in the leafy borders. The tops of the round lilac bushes had a sprinkling of white and purple—a sign that their flowers were ready to open. The foliage of the birch avenue was all transparent in the light of the setting sun. In the veranda there was shade and freshness. The evening dew was sure to be heavy in the grass. Out of doors beyond the garden the last sounds of day were audible, and the noise of the sheep and cattle, as they were driven home. Níkon, the half-witted boy, was driving his water-cart along the path outside the veranda, and a cold stream of water from the sprinkler made dark circles on the mould round the stems and supports of the dahlias. In our veranda the polished samovar shone and hissed on the white table-cloth; there were cracknels and biscuits and cream on the table. Kátya was busy washing the cups with her plump hands. I was too hungry after bathing to wait for tea, and was eating bread with thick fresh cream. I was wearing a gingham blouse with loose sleeves, and my hair, still wet, was covered with a kerchief. Kátya saw him first, even before he came in.

'You, Sergéy Mikháylych!' she cried. 'Why, we were just talking about you.'

I got up, meaning to go and change my dress, but he caught me just by the door.

'Why stand on such ceremony in the country?' he said, looking with a smile at the kerchief on my head. 'You don't mind the presence of your butler, and I am really the same to you as Grigóri is.' But I felt just then that he was looking at me in a way quite unlike Grigóri's way, and I was uncomfortable.

'I shall come back at once,' I said, as I left them.

'But what is wrong?' he called out after me; 'it's just the dress of a young peasant woman.'

'How strangely he looked at me!' I said to myself as I was quickly changing upstairs. 'Well, I'm glad he has come; things will be more lively.' After a look in the glass I ran gaily downstairs and into the veranda; I was out of breath and did not disguise my haste. He was sitting at the table, talking to Kátya about our affairs. He glanced at me and smiled; then he went on talking. From what he said it appeared that our affairs were in capital shape: it was now possible for us, after spending the summer in the country, to go either to Petersburg for Sónya's education, or abroad.

'If only you would go abroad with us—' said Kátya; 'without you we shall be quite lost there.'

'Oh, I should like to go round the world with you,' he said, half in jest and half in earnest.

'All right,' I said; 'let us start off and go round the world.'

He smiled and shook his head.

'What about my mother? What about my business?' he said. 'But that's not the question just now: I want to know how you have been spending your time. Not depressed again, I hope?'

When I told him that I had been busy and not bored during his absence, and when Kátya confirmed my report, he praised me as if he had a right to do so, and his words and looks were kind, as they might have been to a child. I felt obliged to tell him, in detail and with perfect frankness, all my good actions, and to confess, as if I were in church, all that he might disapprove of. The evening was so fine that we stayed in the veranda after tea was cleared away; and the conversation interested me so much that I did not notice how we ceased by degrees to hear any sound of the servants indoors. The scent of flowers grew stronger and came from all sides; the grass was drenched with dew; a nightingale struck up in a lilac bush close by and then stopped on hearing our voices; the starry sky seemed to come down lower over our heads.

It was growing dusk, but I did not notice it till a bat suddenly and silently flew in beneath the veranda awning and began to flutter round my white shawl. I shrank back against the wall and nearly cried out; but the bat as silently and swiftly dived out from under the awning and disappeared in the half-darkness of the garden.

'How fond I am of this place of yours!' he said, changing the conversation; 'I wish I could spend all my life here, sitting in this veranda.'

'Well, do then!' said Kátya.

'That's all very well,' he said, 'but life won't sit still.'

'Why don't you marry?' asked Kátya; 'you would make an excellent husband.'

'Because I like sitting still?' and he laughed. 'No, Katerína Kárlovna, too late for you and me to marry. People have long ceased to think of me as a marrying man, and I am even surer of it myself; and I declare I have felt quite comfortable since the matter was settled.'

It seemed to me that he said this in an unnaturally persuasive way.

'Nonsense!' said Kátya; 'a man of thirty-six makes out that he is too old!'

'Too old indeed,' he went on, 'when all one wants is to sit still. For a man who is going to marry that's not enough. Just you ask her,' he added, nodding at me; 'people of her age should marry, and you and I can rejoice in their happiness.'

The sadness and constraint latent in his voice was not lost upon me. He was silent for a little, and neither Kátya nor I spoke.

'Well, just fancy,' he went on, turning a little on his seat; 'suppose that by some mischance I married a girl of seventeen, Másha, if you like—I mean, Márya Alexándrovna. The instance is good; I am glad it turned up; there could not be a better instance.'

I laughed; but I could not understand why he was glad, or what it was that had turned up.

'Just tell me honestly, with your hand on your heart,' he said, turning as if playfully to me, 'would it not be a misfortune for you to unite your life with that of an old worn-out man who only wants to sit still, whereas Heaven knows what wishes are fermenting in that heart of yours?'

I felt uncomfortable and was silent, not knowing how to answer him.

'I am not making you a proposal, you know,' he said, laughing; 'but am I really the kind of husband you dream of when walking alone in the avenue at twilight? It would be a misfortune, would it not?'

'No, not a misfortune,' I began.

'But a bad thing,' he ended my sentence.

'Perhaps; but I may be mistaken . . .' He interrupted me again.

'There, you see! She is quite right, and I am grateful to her for her frankness, and very glad to have had this conversation. And there is something else to be said'—he added: 'for me too it would be a very great misfortune.'

'How odd you are! You have not changed in the least,' said Kátya, and then left the veranda, to order supper to be served.

When she had gone, we were both silent and all was still around us, but for one exception. A nightingale, which had sung last night by fitful snatches, now flooded the garden with a steady stream of song, and was soon answered by another from the dell below, which had not sung till that evening. The nearer bird stopped and seemed to listen for a moment, and then broke out again still louder than before, pouring out his song in piercing long-drawn cadences. There was a regal calm in the birds' voices, as they floated through the realm of night which belongs to those birds and not to man. The gardener walked past to his sleeping-quarters in the greenhouse, and the noise of his heavy boots grew fainter and fainter along the path. Someone whistled twice sharply at the foot of the hill; and then all was still again. The rustling of leaves could just be heard; the veranda awning flapped; a faint perfume, floating in the air, came down on the veranda and filled it. I felt silence awkward after what had been said, but what to say I did not know. I looked at him. His eyes, bright in the half-darkness, turned towards me.

'How good life is!' he said.

I sighed, I don't know why.

'Well?' he asked.

'Life is good,' I repeated after him.

Again we were silent, and again I felt uncomfortable. I could not help fancying that I had wounded him by agreeing that he was old; and I wished to comfort him but did not know how.

'Well, I must be saying good-bye,' he said, rising; 'my mother expects me for supper; I have hardly seen her all day.'

'I meant to play you the new sonata,' I said.

'That must wait,' he replied; and I thought that he spoke coldly.

'Good-bye.'

I felt still more certain that I had wounded him, and I was sorry. Kátya and I went to the steps to see him off and stood for a while in the open, looking along the road where he had disappeared from view. When we ceased to hear the sound of his horse's hoofs, I walked round the house to the veranda, and again, sat looking into the garden; and all I wished to see and hear, I still saw and heard for a long time in the dewy mist filled with the sounds of night.

He came a second time, and a third; and the awkwardness arising from that strange conversation passed away entirely, never to return. During that whole summer he came two or three times a week; and I grew so accustomed to his presence, that, when he failed to come for some time, I missed him and felt angry with him, and thought he was behaving badly in deserting me. He treated me like a boy whose company he liked, asked me questions, invited the most cordial frankness on my part, gave me advice and encouragement, or sometimes scolded and checked me. But in spite of his constant effort to keep on my level, I was aware that behind the part of him which I could understand there remained an entire region of mystery, into which he did not consider it necessary to admit me; and this fact did much to preserve my respect for him and his attraction for me. I knew from Kátya and from our neighbours that he had not only to care for his old mother with whom he lived, and to manage his own estate and our affairs, but was also responsible for some public business which was the source of serious worries; but what view he took of all this, what were his convictions, plans, and hopes, I could not in the least find out from him. Whenever I turned the conversation to his affairs, he frowned in a way peculiar to himself and seemed to imply, 'Please stop! That is no business of yours;' and then he changed the subject. This hurt me at first; but I soon grew accustomed to confining our talk to my affairs, and felt this to be quite natural.

There was another thing which displeased me at first and then became pleasant to me. This was his complete indifference and even contempt for my personal appearance. Never by word or look did he imply that I was pretty; on the contrary, he frowned and laughed, whenever the word was applied to me in his presence. He even liked to find fault with my looks and tease me about them. On special days Kátya liked to dress me out in fine clothes and to arrange my hair effectively; but my finery met only with mockery from him, which pained kind-hearted Kátya and at first disconcerted me. She had made up her mind that he admired me; and she could not understand how a man could help wishing a woman whom he admired to appear to the utmost advantage. But I soon understood what he wanted. He wished to make sure that I had not a trace of affectation. And when I understood this I was really quite free from affectation in the clothes I wore, or the arrangement of my hair, or my movements; but a very obvious form of affectation took its place—an affectation of simplicity, at a time when I could not yet be really simple. That he loved me, I knew; but I did not yet ask myself whether he loved me as a child or as a woman. I valued his love; I felt that he thought me better than all other young women in the world, and I could not help wishing him to go on being deceived about me. Without wishing to deceive him, I did deceive him, and I became better myself while deceiving him. I felt it a better and worthier course to show him the good points of my heart and mind than of my body. My hair, hands, face, ways—all these, whether good or bad, he had appraised at once and knew so well, that I could add nothing to my external appearance except the wish to deceive him. But my mind and heart he did not know, because he loved them, and because they were in the very process of growth and development; and on this point I could and did deceive him. And how easy I felt in his company, once I understood this clearly! My causeless bashfulness and awkward movements completely disappeared. Whether he saw me from in front, or in profile, sitting or standing, with my hair up or my hair down, I felt that he knew me from head to foot, and I fancied, was satisfied with me as I was. If, contrary to his habit, he had suddenly said to me as other people did, that I had a pretty face, I believe that I should not have liked it at all. But, on the other hand, how light and happy my heart was when, after I had said something, he looked hard at me and said, hiding emotion under a mask of raillery:

'Yes, there *is* something in you! you are a fine girl—that I must tell you.'

And for what did I receive such rewards, which filled my heart with pride and joy? Merely for saying that I felt for old Grigóri in his love for his little granddaughter; or because the reading of some poem or novel moved me to tears; or because I liked Mozart better than Schulhof. And I was surprised at my own quickness in guessing what was good and worthy of love, when I certainly did not know then what *was* good and worthy to be loved. Most of my former tastes and habits did not please him; and a mere look of his, or a twitch of his eyebrow was enough to show that he did not like what I was trying to say; and I felt at once that my own standard was changed. Sometimes, when he was about to give me a piece of advice, I seemed to know beforehand what he would say. When he looked in my face and asked me a question, his very look would draw out of me the answer he wanted. All my thoughts and feelings of that time were not really mine: they were his thoughts and feelings, which had suddenly become mine and passed into my life and lighted it up. Quite unconsciously I began to look at everything with different eyes—at Kátya and the servants and Sónya and myself and my occupations. Books, which I used to read merely to escape boredom, now became one of the chief pleasures of my life, merely because he brought me the books and we read and discussed them together. The lessons I gave to Sónya had been a burdensome obligation which I forced myself to go through from a sense of duty; but, after he was present at a lesson, it became a joy to me to watch Sónya's progress. It used to seem to me an impossibility to learn a whole piece of music by heart; but now, when I knew that he would hear it and might praise it, I would play a single movement forty times over without stopping, till poor Katya stuffed her ears with cotton-wool, while I was still not weary of it. The same old sonatas seemed quite different in their expression, and came out quite changed and much improved. Even Kátya, whom I knew and loved like a second self, became different in my eyes. I now understood for the first time that she was not in the least bound to be the mother, friend, and slave that she was to us. Now I appreciated all the self-sacrifice and devotion of this affectionate creature, and all my obligations to her; and I began to love her even better. It was he too who taught me to take quite a new view of our serfs and servants and maids. It is an absurd confession to make—but I had spent seventeen years among these people and yet knew less about them than about strangers whom I had never seen; it had never once occurred to me that they had their affections and wishes and sorrows, just as I had. Our garden and woods and fields, which I had known so long, became suddenly new and beautiful to me. He was right in saying that the only certain happiness in life is to live for others. At the time his words seemed to me strange, and I did not understand them; but by degrees, this became a conviction with me, without thinking about it. He revealed to me a whole new world of joys in the present, without changing anything in my life, without adding anything except himself to each impression in my mind. All that had surrounded me from childhood without saying anything to me, suddenly came to life. The mere sight of him made everything begin to speak and press for admittance to my heart, filling it with happiness.

Often during that summer, when I went upstairs to my room and lay down on my bed, the old unhappiness of spring with its desires and hopes for the future gave place to a passionate happiness in the present. Unable to sleep, I often got up and sat on Kátya's bed, and told her how perfectly happy I was, though I now realize that this was quite unnecessary, as she could see it for herself. But she told me that she was quite content and perfectly happy, and kissed me. I believed her—it seemed to me so necessary and just that everyone should be happy. But Kátya could think of sleep too; and sometimes, pretending to be angry, she drove me from her bed and went to sleep, while I turned over and over in my mind all that made me so happy. Sometimes I got up and said my prayers over again, praying in my own words and thanking God for all the happiness he had given me.

All was quiet in the room; there was only the even breathing of Kátya in her sleep, and the ticking of the clock by her bed, while I turned from side to side and whispered words of prayer, or crossed myself and kissed the cross round my neck. The door was shut and the windows shuttered; perhaps a fly or gnat hung buzzing in the air. I felt a wish never to leave that room—a wish that dawn might never come, that my present frame of mind might never change. I felt that my dreams and thoughts and prayers were live things, living there in the dark with me, hovering about my bed, and standing over me. And every thought was his thought, and every feeling his feeling. I did not know yet that this was love; I thought that things might go on so for ever, and that this feeling involved no consequences.

III

One day when the corn was being carried, I went with Kátya and Sónya to our favourite seat in the garden, in the shade of the lime-trees and above the dell, beyond which the fields and woods lay open before us. It was three days since Sergéy Mikháylych had been to see us; we were expecting him, all the more because our bailiff reported that he had promised to visit the harvest-field. At two o'clock we saw him ride on to the rye-field. With a smile and a glance at me, Kátya ordered peaches and cherries, of which he was very fond, to be brought; then she lay down on the bench and began to doze. I tore off a crooked flat lime-tree branch, which made my hand wet with its juicy leaves and juicy bark. Then I fanned Kátya with it and went on with my book, breaking off from time to time, to look at the field-path along which he must come. Sónya was making a dolls' house at the root of an old lime-tree. The day was sultry, windless, and steaming; the clouds were packing and growing blacker; all morning a thunderstorm had been gathering, and I felt restless, as I always did before thunder. But by afternoon the clouds began to part, the sun sailed out into a clear sky, and only in one quarter was there a faint rumbling. A single heavy cloud, louring above the horizon and mingling with the dust from the fields, was rent from time to time by pale zigzags of lightning which ran down to the ground. It was clear that for to-day the storm would pass off, with us at all events. The road beyond the garden was visible in places, and we could see a procession of high creaking carts slowly moving along it with their load of sheaves, while the empty carts rattled at a faster pace to meet them, with swaying legs and shirts fluttering in them. The thick dust neither blew away nor settled down—it stood still beyond the fence, and we could see it through the transparent foliage of the garden trees. A little farther off, in the stackyard, the same voices and the same creaking of wheels were audible; and the same yellow sheaves that had moved slowly past the fence were now flying aloft, and I could see the oval stacks gradually rising higher, and their conspicuous pointed tops, and the labourers swarming upon them. On the dusty field in front more carts were moving and more yellow sheaves were visible; and the noise of the carts, with the sound of talking and singing, came to us from a distance. At one side the bare stubble, with strips of fallow covered with wormwood, came more and more into view. Lower down, to the right, the gay dresses of the women were visible, as they bent down and swung their arms to bind the sheaves. Here the bare stubble looked untidy; but the disorder was cleared by degrees, as the pretty sheaves were ranged at close intervals. It seemed as if summer had suddenly turned to autumn before my eyes. The dust and heat were everywhere, except in our favourite nook in the garden; and everywhere, in this heat and dust and under the burning sun, the labourers carried on their heavy task with talk and noise.

Meanwhile Kátya slept so sweetly on our shady bench, beneath her white cambric handkerchief, the black juicy cherries glistened so temptingly on the plate, our dresses were so clean and fresh, the water in the jug was so bright with rainbow colours in the sun, and I felt so happy! 'How can I help it?' I thought; 'am I to blame for being happy? And how can I share my happiness? How and to whom can I surrender all myself and all my happiness?'

By this time the sun had sunk behind the tops of the birch avenue, the dust was settling on the fields, the distance became clearer and brighter in the slanting light. The clouds had dispersed altogether; I could see through the trees the thatch of three new corn-stacks. The labourers came down off the stacks; the carts hurried past, evidently for the last time, with a loud noise of shouting; the women, with rakes over their shoulders and straw-bands in their belts, walked home past us, singing loudly; and still there was no sign of Sergéy Mikháylych, though I had seen him ride down the hill long ago. Suddenly he appeared upon the avenue, coming from a quarter where I was not looking for him. He had walked round by the dell. He came quickly towards me, with his hat off and radiant with high spirits. Seeing that Kátya was asleep, he bit his lip, closed his eyes, and advanced on tiptoe; I saw at once that he was in that peculiar mood of causeless merriment which I always delighted to see in him, and which we called 'wild ecstasy'. He was just like a schoolboy playing truant; his whole figure, from head to foot, breathed content, happiness, and boyish frolic.

'Well, young violet, how are you? All right?' he said in a whisper, coming up to me and taking my hand. Then, in answer to my question, 'Oh, I'm splendid to-day, I feel like a boy of thirteen—I want to play at horses and climb trees.'

'Is it wild ecstasy?' I asked, looking into his laughing eyes, and feeling that the 'wild ecstasy' was infecting me.

'Yes,' he answered, winking and checking a smile. 'But I don't see why you need hit Katerína Kárlovna on the nose.'

With my eyes on him I had gone on waving the branch, without noticing that I had knocked the handkerchief off Kátya's face and was now brushing her with the leaves. I laughed.

'She will say she was awake all the time,' I whispered, as if not to awake Kátya; but that was not my real reason—it was only that I liked to whisper to him.

He moved his lips in imitation of me, pretending that my voice was too low for him to hear. Catching sight of the dish of cherries, he pretended to steal it, and carried it off to Sónya under the lime-tree, where he sat down on her dolls. Sónya was angry at first, but he soon made his peace with her by starting a game, to see which of them could eat cherries faster.

'If you like, I will send for more cherries,' I said; 'or let us go ourselves.'

He took the dish and set the dolls on it, and we all three started for the orchard. Sónya ran behind us, laughing and pulling at his coat, to make him surrender the dolls. He gave them up and then turned to me, speaking more seriously.

'You really are a violet,' he said, still speaking low, though there was no longer any fear of waking anybody; 'when I came to you out of all that dust and heat and toil, I positively smelt violets at once. But not the sweet violet—you know, that early dark violet that smells of melting snow and spring grass.'

'Is harvest going on well?' I asked, in order to hide the happy agitation which his words produced in me.

'First-rate! Our people are always splendid. The more you know them, the better you like them.'

'Yes,' I said; 'before you came I was watching them from the garden, and suddenly I felt ashamed to be so comfortable myself while they were hard at work, and so . . .'

He interrupted me, with a kind but grave look: 'Don't talk like that, my dear; it is too sacred a matter to talk of lightly. God forbid that you should use fine phrases about that!'

'But it is only to *you* I say this.'

'All right, I understand. But what about those cherries?'

The orchard was locked, and no gardener to be seen: he had sent them all off to help with the harvest. Sónya ran to fetch the key. But he would not wait for her: climbing up a corner of the wall, he raised the net and jumped down on the other side.

His voice came over the wall—'If you want some, give me the dish.'

'No,' I said; 'I want to pick for myself. I shall fetch the key; Sónya won't find it.'

But suddenly I felt that I must see what he was doing there and what he looked like—that I must watch his movements while he supposed that no one saw him. Besides I was simply unwilling just then to lose sight of him for a single minute. Running on tiptoe through the nettles to the other side of the orchard where the wall was lower, I mounted on an empty cask, till the top of the wall was on a level with my waist, and then leaned over into the orchard. I looked at the gnarled old trees, with their broad dented leaves and the ripe black cherries hanging straight and heavy among the foliage; then I pushed my head under the net, and from under the knotted bough of an old cherry-tree I caught sight of Sergéy Mikháylych. He evidently thought that I had gone away and that no one was watching him. With his hat off and his eyes shut, he was sitting on the fork of an old tree and carefully rolling into a ball a lump of cherry-tree gum. Suddenly he shrugged his shoulders, opened his eyes, muttered something, and smiled. Both words and smile were so unlike him that I felt ashamed of myself for eavesdropping. It seemed to me that he had said, 'Másha!' 'Impossible,' I thought. 'Darling Másha!' he said again, in a lower and more tender tone. There was no possible doubt about the two words this time. My heart beat hard, and such a passionate joy—illicit joy, as I felt—took hold of me, that I clutched at the wall, fearing to fall and betray myself. Startled by the sound of my movement, he looked round—he dropped his eyes instantly, and his face turned red, even scarlet, like a child's. He tried to speak, but in vain; again and again his face positively flamed up. Still he smiled as he looked at me, and I smiled too. Then his whole face grew radiant with happiness. He had ceased to be the old uncle who spoiled or scolded me; he was a man on my level, who loved and feared me as I loved and feared him. We looked at one another without speaking. But suddenly he frowned; the smile and light in his eyes disappeared, and he resumed his cold paternal tone, just as if we were doing something wrong and he was repenting and calling on me to repent.

'You had better get down, or you will hurt yourself,' he said; 'and do put your hair straight; just think what you look like!'

'What makes him pretend? what makes him want to give me pain?' I thought in my vexation. And the same instant brought an irresistible desire to upset his composure again and test my power over him.

'No,' I said; 'I mean to pick for myself.' I caught hold of the nearest branch and climbed to the top of the wall; then, before he had time to catch me, I jumped down on the other side.

'What foolish things you do!' he muttered, flushing again

and trying to hide his confusion under a pretence of annoyance; 'you might really have hurt yourself. But how do you mean to get out of this?'

He was even more confused than before, but this time his confusion frightened rather than pleased me. It infected me too and made me blush; avoiding his eye and not knowing what to say, I began to pick cherries though I had nothing to put them in. I reproached myself, I repented of what I had done, I was frightened; I felt that I had lost his good opinion for ever by my folly. Both of us were silent and embarrassed. From this difficult situation Sónya rescued us by running back with the key in her hand. For some time we both addressed our conversation to her and said nothing to each other. When we returned to Kátya, who assured us that she had never been asleep and was listening all the time, I calmed down, and he tried to drop into his fatherly patronizing manner again, but I was not taken in by it. A discussion which we had had some days before came back clear before me.

Kátya had been saying that it was easier for a man to be in love and declare his love than for a woman.

'A man may say that he is in love, and a woman can't,' she said.

'I disagree,' said he; 'a man has no business to say, and can't say, that he is in love.'

'Why not?' I asked.

'Because it never can be true. What sort of a revelation is that, that a man is in love? A man seems to think that whenever he says the word, something will go pop!—that some miracle will be worked, signs and wonders, with all the big guns firing at once! In my opinion,' he went on, 'whoever solemnly brings out the words "I love you" is either deceiving himself or, which is even worse, deceiving others.'

'Then how is a woman to know that a man is in love with her, unless he tells her?' asked Kátya.

'That I don't know,' he answered; 'every man has his own way of telling things. If the feeling exists, it will out somehow. But when I read novels, I always fancy the crestfallen look of Lieut. Strélsky or Alfred, when he says, "I love you, Eleanora", and expects something wonderful to happen at once, and no change at all takes place in either of them—their eyes and their noses and their whole selves remain exactly as they were.'

Even then I had felt that this banter covered something serious that had reference to myself. But Kátya resented his disrespectful treatment of the heroes in novels.

'You are never serious,' she said; 'but tell me truthfully, have you never yourself told a woman that you loved her?'

'Never, and never gone down on one knee,' he answered, laughing; 'and never will.'

This conversation I now recalled, and I reflected that there was no need for him to tell me that he loved me. 'I know that he loves me,' I thought, 'and all his endeavours to seem indifferent will not change my opinion.'

He said little to me throughout the evening, but in every word he said to Kátya and Sónya and in every look and movement of his I saw love and felt no doubt of it. I was only vexed and sorry for him, that he thought it necessary still to hide his feelings and pretend coldness, when it was all so clear, and when it would have been so simple and easy to be boundlessly happy. But my jumping down to him in the orchard weighed on me like a crime. I kept feeling that he would cease to respect me and was angry with me.

After tea I went to the piano, and he followed me.

'Play me something—it is long since I heard you,' he said, catching me up in the parlour.

'I was just going to,' I said. Then I looked straight in his face and said quickly, 'Sergéy Mikháylych, you are not angry with me, are you?'

'What for?' he asked.

'For not obeying you this afternoon,' I said, blushing.

He understood me: he shook his head and made a grimace, which implied that I deserved a scolding but that he did not feel able to give it

'So it's all right, and we are friends again?' I said, sitting down at the piano.

'Of course!' he said.

In the drawing-room, a large lofty room, there were only two lighted candles on the piano, the rest of the room remaining in half-darkness. Outside the open windows the summer night was bright. All was silent, except when the sound of Kátya's footsteps in the unlighted parlour was heard occasionally, or when his horse, which was tied up under the window, snorted or stamped his hoof on the burdocks that grew there. He sat behind me, where I could not see him; but everywhere— in the half-darkness of the room, in every sound, in myself—I felt his presence. Every look, every movement of his, though I could not see them, found an echo in my heart. I played a sonata of Mozart's which he had brought me and which I had learnt in his presence and for him. I was not thinking at all of what I was playing, but I believe that I played it well, and I thought that he was pleased. I was conscious of his pleasure, and conscious too, though I never looked at him, of the gaze fixed on me from behind. Still moving my fingers mechanically, I turned round quite involuntarily and looked at him. The night had grown brighter, and his head stood out on a background of darkness. He was sitting with his head propped on his hands, and his eyes shone as they gazed at me. Catching his look, I smiled and stopped playing. He smiled too and shook his head reproach-fully at the music, for me to go on. When I stopped, the moon had grown brighter and was riding high in the heavens; and the faint light of the candles was supplemented by a new silvery light which came in through the windows and fell on the floor. Kátya called out that it was really too bad—that I had stopped at the best part of the piece, and that I was playing badly. But he declared that I had never played so well; and then he began to walk about the rooms—through the drawing-room to the un-lighted parlour and back again to the drawing-room, and each time he looked at me and smiled. I smiled too; I wanted even to laugh with no reason; I was so happy at something that had happened that very day. Kátya and I were standing by the piano; and each time that he vanished through the drawing-room door, I started kissing her in my favourite place, the soft part of her neck under the chin; and each time he came back, I made a solemn face and refrained with difficulty from laughing.

'What is the matter with her to-day?' Kátya asked him.

He only smiled at me without answering; he knew what was the matter with me.

'Just look what a night it is!' he called out from the parlour, where he had stopped by the open French window looking into the garden.

We joined him; and it really was such a night as I have never seen since. The full moon shone above the house and behind us, so that we could not see it, and half the shadow, thrown by the roof and pillars of the house and by the veranda awning, lay slanting and foreshortened on the gravel-path and the strip of turf beyond. Everything else was bright and saturated with the silver of the dew and the moonlight. The broad garden-path, on one side of which the shadows of the dahlias and their supports lay aslant, all bright and cold, and shining on the inequalities of the gravel, ran on till it vanished in the mist. Through the trees the roof of the greenhouse shone bright, and a growing mist rose from the dell. The lilac-bushes, already partly leafless, were all bright to the centre. Each flower was distinguishable apart, and all were drenched with dew. In the avenues light and shade were so mingled that they looked, not like paths and trees but like transparent houses, swaying and moving. To our right, in the shadow of the house, everything was black, indistinguishable, and uncanny. But all the brighter for the surrounding darkness was the top of a poplar, with a fantastic crown of leaves, which for some strange reason remained there close to the house, towering into the bright light, instead of flying away into the dim distance, into the retreating dark-blue of the sky.

'Let us go for a walk,' I said.

Kátya agreed, but said I must put on goloshes.

'I don't want them, Kátya,' I said; 'Sergéy Mikháylych will give me his arm.'

As if that would prevent me from wetting my feet! But to us three this seemed perfectly natural at the time. Though he never used to offer me his arm, I now took it of my own accord, and he saw nothing strange in it. We all went down from the veranda together. That whole world, that sky, that garden, that air, were different from those that I knew.

We were walking along an avenue, and it seemed to me, whenever I looked ahead, that we could go no farther in the same direction, that the world of the possible ended there, and that the whole scene must remain fixed for ever in its beauty. But we still moved on, and the magic wall kept parting to let us in; and still we found the familiar garden with trees and paths and withered leaves. And we were really walking along the paths, treading on patches of light and shade; and a withered leaf was really crackling under my foot, and a live twig brushing my face. And that was really he, walking steadily and slowly at my side, and carefully supporting my arm; and that was really Kátya walking beside us with her creaking shoes. And that must be the moon in the sky, shining down on us through the motionless branches.

But at each step the magic wall closed up again behind us and in front, and I ceased to believe in the possibility of advancing farther—I ceased to believe in the reality of it all.

'Oh, there's a frog!' cried Kátya.

'Who said that? and why?' I thought. But then I realized it was Kátya, and that she was afraid of frogs. Then I looked at the ground and saw a little frog which gave a jump and then stood still in front of me, while its tiny shadow was reflected on the shining clay of the path.

'You're not afraid of frogs, are you?' he asked.

I turned and looked at him. Just where we were there was a gap of one tree in the lime-avenue, and I could see his face clearly—it was so handsome and so happy!

Though he had spoken of my fear of frogs, I knew that he meant to say, 'I love you, my dear one!' 'I love you, I love you' was repeated by his look, by his arm; the light, the shadow, and the air all repeated the same words.

We had gone all round the garden. Kátya's short steps had kept up with us, but now she was tired and out of breath. She said it was time to go in; and I felt very sorry for her. 'Poor thing!' I thought; 'why does not she feel as we do? why are we not all young and happy, like this night and like him and me?'

We went in, but it was a long time before he went away, though the cocks had crowed, and everyone in the house was asleep, and his horse, tethered under the window, snorted continually and stamped his hoof on the burdocks. Kátya never reminded us of the hour, and we sat on talking of the merest trifles and not thinking of the time, till it was past two. The cocks were crowing for the third time and the dawn was breaking when he rode away. He said good-bye as usual and made no special allusion; but I knew that from that day he was mine, and that I should never lose him now. As soon as I had confessed to myself that I loved him, I took Kátya into my confidence. She rejoiced in the news and was touched by my telling her; but she was actually able—poor thing!—to go to bed and sleep! For me, I walked for a long, long time about the veranda; then I went down to the garden, where, recalling each word, each movement, I walked along the same avenues through which I had walked with him. I did not sleep at all that night, and saw sunrise and early dawn for the first time in my life. And never again did I see such a night and such a morning. 'Only why does he not tell me plainly that he loves me?' I thought; 'what makes him invent obstacles and call himself old, when all is so simple and so splendid? What makes him waste this golden time which may never return? Let him say "I love you"—say it in plain words; let him take my hand in his and bend over it and say "I love you". Let him blush and look down before me; and then I will tell him all. No! not tell him, but throw my arms round him and press close to him and weep.' But then a thought came to me—'What if I am mistaken and he does not love me?'

I was startled by this fear—God knows where it might have led me. I recalled his embarrassment and mine, when I jumped down to him in the orchard; and my heart grew very heavy. Tears gushed from my eyes, and I began to pray. A strange thought occurred to me, calming me and bringing hope with it. I resolved to begin fasting on that day, to take the Communion on my birthday, and on that same day to be betrothed to him.

How this result would come to pass I had no idea; but from that moment I believed and felt sure it would be so. The dawn had fully come and the labourers were getting up when I went back to my room.

IV

The Fast of the Assumption falling in August, no one in the house was surprised by my intention of fasting.

During the whole of the week he never once came to see us; but, far from being surprised or vexed or made uneasy by his absence, I was glad of it—I did not expect him until my birthday. Each day during the week I got up early. While the horses were being harnessed, I walked in the garden alone, turning over in my mind the sins of the day before, and considering what I must do to-day, so as to be satisfied with my day and not spoil it by a single sin. It seemed so easy to me then to abstain from sin altogether; only a trifling effort seemed necessary. When the horses came round, I got into the carriage with Kátya or one of the maids, and we drove to the church two miles away. While entering the church, I always recalled the prayer for those who 'come unto the Temple in the fear of God', and tried to get just that flame of mind when mounting the two grass-grown steps up to the building. At that hour there were not more than a dozen worshippers—household servants or peasant women keeping the Fast. They bowed to me, and I returned their bows with studied humility. Then, with what seemed to me a great effort of courage, I went myself and got candles from the man who kept them, an old soldier and an Elder; and I placed the candles before the icons. Through the central door of the altar-screen I could see the altar-cloth which my mother had worked; on the screen were the two angels which had seemed so big to me when I was little, and the dove with a golden halo which had fascinated me long ago. Behind the choir stood the old battered font, where I had been christened myself and had stood godmother to so many of the servants' children. The old priest came out, wearing a cope made of the pall that had covered my father's coffin, and began to read in the same voice that I had heard all my life—at services held in our house, at Sónya's christening, at memorial services for my father, and at my mother's funeral. The same old quavering voice of the deacon rose in the choir; and the same old woman, whom I could remember at every service in that church, crouched by the wall, fixing her streaming eyes on an icon in the choir, pressing her folded fingers against her faded kerchief, and muttering with her tooth-less gums. And these objects were no longer merely curious to me, merely interesting from old recollections—each had become important and sacred in my eyes and seemed charged with profound meaning. I listened to each word of the prayers and tried to suit my feeling to it; and if I failed to understand, I prayed silently that God would enlighten me, or made up a prayer of my own in place of what I had failed to catch. When the penitential prayers were repeated, I recalled my past life, and that innocent childish past seemed to me so black when compared to the present brightness of my soul, that I wept and was horrified at myself; but I felt too that all those sins would be forgiven, and that if my sins had been even greater, my repentance would be all the sweeter. At the end of the service when the priest said, 'The blessing of the Lord be upon you!' I seemed to feel an immediate sensation of physical well-being, of a mysterious light and warmth that instantly filled my heart. The service over, the priest came and asked me whether he should come to our house to say Mass, and what hour would suit me; and I thanked him for the suggestion, intended, as I thought, to please me, but said that I would come to church instead, walking or driving.

'Is that not too much trouble?' he asked. And I was at a loss for an answer, fearing to commit a sin of pride.

After the Mass, if Kátya was not with me, I always sent the carriage home and walked back alone, bowing humbly to all who passed, and trying to find an opportunity of giving help or advice. I was eager to sacrifice myself for someone, to help in lifting a fallen cart, to rock a child's cradle, to give up the path to others by stepping into the mud. One evening I heard the bailiff report to Kátya that Simon, one of our serfs, had come to beg some boards to make a coffin for his daughter, and a rouble to pay the priest for the funeral; the bailiff had given what he asked. 'Are they as poor as that?' I asked. 'Very poor, Miss,' the bailiff answered; 'they have no salt to their food.' My heart ached to hear this, and yet I felt a kind of pleasure too. Pretending to Kátya that I was merely going for a walk, I ran upstairs, got out all my money (it was very little but it was all I had), crossed myself, and started off alone, through the veranda and the garden, on my way to Simon's hut. It stood at the end of the village, and no one saw me as I went up to the window, placed the money on the sill, and tapped on the pane. Someone came out, making the door creak, and hailed me; but I hurried home, cold and shaking with fear like a criminal. Kátya asked where I had been and what was the matter with me; but I did not answer, and did not even understand what she was saying. Everything suddenly seemed to me so petty and insignificant. I locked myself up in my own room, and walked up and down alone for a long time, unable to do anything, unable to think, unable to understand my own feelings. I thought of the joy of the whole family, and of what they would say of their benefactor; and I felt sorry that I had not given them the money myself. I thought too of what Sergéy Mikháylych would say, if he knew what I had done; and I was glad to think that no one would ever find out. I was so happy, and I felt myself and everyone else so bad, and yet was so kindly disposed to myself and to all the world, that the thought of death came to me as a dream of happiness. I smiled and prayed and wept, and felt at that moment a burning passion of love for all the world, myself included. Between services I used to read the Gospel; and the book became more and more intelligible to me, and the story of that divine life simpler and more touching; and the depths of thought and feeling I found in studying it became more awful and impenetrable. On the other hand, how clear and simple everything seemed to me when I rose from the study of this book and looked again on life around me and reflected on it! It was so difficult, I felt, to lead a bad life, and so simple to love everyone and be loved. All were so kind and gentle to me; even Sónya, whose lessons I had not broken off, was quite different—trying to understand and please me and not to vex me. Everyone treated me as I treated them. Thinking over my enemies, of whom I must ask pardon before confession, I could only remember one—one of our neighbours, a girl, whom I had made fun of in company a year ago, and who had ceased to visit us. I wrote to her, confessing my fault and asking her forgiveness. She replied that she forgave me and wished me to forgive her. I cried for joy over her simple words, and saw in them, at the time, a deep and touching feeling. My old nurse cried, when I asked her to forgive me. 'What makes them all so kind to me? what have I done to deserve their love?' I asked myself. Sergéy Mikháylych would come into my mind, and I thought for long about him. I could not help it, and I did not consider these thoughts sinful. But my thoughts of him were quite different from what they had been on the night when I first realized that I loved him: he seemed to me now like a second self, and became a part of every plan for the future. The inferiority which I had always felt in his presence had vanished entirely: I felt myself his equal, and could understand him thoroughly from the moral elevation I had reached. What had seemed strange in him was now quite clear to me. Now I could see what he meant by saying that to live for others was the only true happiness, and I agreed with him perfectly. I believed that our life together would be endlessly happy and untroubled. I looked forward, not to foreign tours or fashionable society or display, but to a quite different scene—a quiet family life in the country, with constant self-sacrifice, constant mutual love, and constant recognition in all things of the kind hand of Providence.

I carried out my plan of taking the Communion on my birthday. When I came back from church that day, my heart was so swelling with happiness that I was afraid of life, afraid of any feeling that might break in on that happiness. We had hardly left the carriage for the steps in front of the house, when there was a sound of wheels on the bridge, and I saw Sergéy Mikháylych drive up in his well-known trap. He congratulated me, and we went together to the parlour. Never since I had known him had I been so much at my ease with him and so self-possessed as on that morning. I felt in myself a whole new world, out of his reach and beyond his comprehension. I was not conscious of the slightest embarrassment in speaking to him. He must have understood the cause of this feeling; for he was tender and gentle beyond his wont and showed a kind of reverent consideration for me. When I made for the piano, he locked it and put the key in his pocket.

'Don't spoil your present mood,' he said, 'you have the sweetest of all music in your soul just now.'

I was grateful for his words, and yet I was not quite pleased at his understanding too easily and clearly what ought to have been an exclusive secret in my heart. At dinner he said that he had come to congratulate me and also to say good-bye; for he must go to Moscow to-morrow. He looked at Kátya as he spoke; but then he stole a glance at me, and I saw that he was afraid he might detect signs of emotion on my face. But I was neither surprised nor agitated; I did not even ask whether he would be long away. I knew he would say this, and I knew that he would not go. How did I know? I cannot explain that to myself now; but on that memorable day it seemed that I knew everything that had been and that would be. It was like a delightful dream, when all that happens seems to have happened already and to be quite familiar, and it will all happen over again, and one knows that it will happen.

He meant to go away immediately after dinner; but, as Kátya was tired after church and went to lie down for a little, he had to wait until she woke up in order to say good-bye to her. The sun shone into the drawing-room, and we went out to the veranda. When we were seated, I began at once, quite calmly, the conversation that was bound to fix the fate of my heart. I began to speak, no sooner and no later, but at the very moment when we sat down, before our talk had taken any turn or colour that might have hindered me from saying what I meant to say. I cannot tell myself where it came from—my coolness and determination and preciseness of expression. It was as if something independent of my will was speaking through my lips. He sat opposite me with his elbows resting on the rails of the veranda; he pulled a lilac-branch towards him and stripped the leaves off it. When I began to speak, he let go the branch and leaned his head on one hand. His attitude might have shown either perfect calmness or strong emotion.

'Why are you going?' I asked, significantly, deliberately, and looking straight at him.

He did not answer at once.

'Business!' he muttered at last and dropped his eyes.

I realized how difficult he found it to lie to me, and in reply to such a frank question.

'Listen,' I said; 'you know what to-day is to me, how important for many reasons. If I question you, it is not to show an interest in your doings (you know that I have become intimate with you and fond of you)– –I ask you this question, because I *must* know the answer. Why are you going?'

'It is very hard for me to tell you the true reason,' he said. 'During this week I have thought much about you and about myself, and have decided that I must go. You understand why; and if you care for me, you will ask no questions.' He put up a hand to rub his forehead and cover his eyes. 'I find it very difficult . . . But you will understand.'

My heart began to beat fast.

'I cannot understand you,' I said; 'I *cannot! You* must tell me; in God's name and for the sake of this day tell me what you please, and I shall hear it with calmness,' I said.

He changed his position, glanced at me, and again drew the lilac-twig towards him.

'Well!' he said, after a short silence in a voice that tried in vain to seem steady, 'it is a foolish business and impossible to put into words, and I feel the difficulty, but I will try to explain it to you,' he added, frowning as if in bodily pain.

'Well?' I said.

'Just imagine the existence of a man—let us call him A— who has left youth far behind, and of a woman whom we may call B, who is young and happy and has seen nothing as yet of life or of the world. Family circumstances of various kinds brought them together, and he grew to love her as a daughter, and had no fear that his love would change its nature.'

He stopped, but I did not interrupt him.

'But he forgot that B was so young, that life was still all a May-game to her,' he went on with a sudden swiftness and determination and without looking at me, 'and that it was easy to fall in love with her in a different way, and that this would amuse her. He made a mistake and was suddenly aware of another feeling, as heavy as remorse, making its way into his heart, and he was afraid. He was afraid that their old friendly relations would be destroyed, and he made up his mind to go away before that happened.' As he said this, he began again to rub his eyes, with a pretence of indifference, and to close them.

'Why was he afraid to love differently?' I asked very low; but I restrained my emotion and spoke in an even voice. He evidently thought that I was not serious; for he answered as if he were hurt.

'You are young, and I am not young. You want amusement, and I want something different. Amuse yourself, if you like, but not with me. If you do, I shall take it seriously; and then I shall be unhappy, and you will repent. That is what A said,' he added; 'however, this is all nonsense; but you understand why I am going. And don't let us continue this conversation. Please not!'

'No! no!' I said, 'we must continue it,' and tears began to tremble in my voice. 'Did he love her, or not?'

He did not answer.

'If he did not love her, why did he treat her as a child and pretend to her?' I asked.

'Yes, A behaved badly,' he interrupted me quickly; 'but it all came to an end and they parted friends.'

'This is horrible! Is there no other ending?' I said with a great effort, and then felt afraid of what I had said.

'Yes, there is,' he said, showing a face full of emotion and looking straight at me. 'There are two different endings. But, for God's sake, listen to me quietly and don't interrupt. Some say'—here he stood up and smiled with a smile that was heavy with pain—'some say that A went off his head, fell passionately in love with B, and told her so. But she only laughed. To her it was all a jest, but to him a matter of life and death.'

I shuddered and tried to interrupt him—tried to say that he must not dare to speak for me; but he checked me, laying his hand on mine.

'Wait!' he said, and his voice shook. 'The other story is that she took pity on him, and fancied, poor child, from her ignorance of the world, that she really could love him, and so consented to be his wife. And he, in his madness, believed it— believed that his whole life could begin anew; but she saw herself that she had deceived him and that he had deceived her. . . . But let us drop the subject finally,' he ended, clearly unable to say more; and then he began to walk up and down in silence before me.

Though he had asked that the subject should be dropped, I saw that his whole soul was hanging on my answer. I tried to speak, but the pain at my heart kept me dumb. I glanced at him—he was pale and his lower lip trembled. I felt sorry for him. With a sudden effort I broke the bonds of silence which had held me fast, and began to speak in a low inward voice, which I feared would break every moment.

'There is a third ending to the story,' I said, and then paused, but he said nothing; 'the third ending is that he did not love her, but hurt her, hurt her, and thought that he was right; and he left her and was actually proud of himself. You have been pretending, not I; I have loved you since the first day we met, loved you,' I repeated, and at the word 'loved' my low inward voice changed, without intention of mine, to a wild cry which frightened me myself.

He stood pale before me, his lip trembled more and more violently, and two tears came out upon his cheeks.

'It is wrong!' I almost screamed, feeling that I was choking with angry unshed tears. 'Why do you do it?' I cried, and got up to leave him.

But he would not let me go. His head was resting on my knees, his lips were kissing my still trembling hands, and his tears were wetting them. 'My God! if I had only known!' he whispered.

'Why? why?' I kept on repeating, but in my heart there was happiness, happiness which had now come back, after so nearly departing for ever.

Five minutes later Sónya was rushing upstairs to Kátya and proclaiming all over the house that Másha intended to marry Sergéy Mikháylych.

V

There were no reasons for putting off our wedding, and neither he nor I wished for delay. Kátya, it is true, thought we ought to go to Moscow, to buy and order wedding-clothes; and his mother tried to insist that, before the wedding, he must set up a new carriage, buy new furniture, and re-paper the whole house. But we two together carried our point, that all these things, if they were really indispensable, should be done afterwards, and that we should be married within a fortnight after my birthday, quietly, without wedding-clothes, without a party, without best men and supper and champagne, and all the other conventional features of a wedding. He told me how dissatisfied his mother was that there should be no band, no mountain of luggage, no renovation of the whole house—so unlike her own marriage which had cost thirty thousand roubles; and he told of the solemn and secret confabulations which she held in her store-room with her housekeeper, Maryúshka, rummaging, the chests and discussing carpets, curtains, and salvers as indispensable conditions of our happiness. At our house Kátya did just the same with my old nurse, Kuzmínichna. It was impossible to treat the matter lightly with Kátya. She was firmly convinced that he and I, when discussing our future, were merely talking the sentimental nonsense natural to people in our position; and that our real future happiness depended on the hemming of table-cloths and napkins and the proper cutting-out and stitching of under-clothing. Several times a day secret information passed between the two houses, to communicate what was going forward in each; and though the external relations between Kátya and his mother were most affectionate, yet a slightly hostile though very subtle diplomacy was already perceptible in their dealings. I now became more intimate with Tatyána Semënovna, the mother of Sergéy Mikháylych, an old-fashioned lady, strict and formal in the management of her household. Her son loved her, and not merely because she was his mother: he thought her the best, cleverest, kindest, and most affectionate woman in the world. She was always kind to us and to me especially, and was glad that her son should be getting married; but when I was with her after our engagement, I always felt that she wished me to understand that, in her opinion, her son might have looked higher, and that it would be as well for me to keep that in mind. I understood her meaning perfectly and thought her quite right.

During that fortnight he and I met every day. He came to dinner regularly and stayed on till midnight. But though he said—and I knew he was speaking the truth—that he had no life apart from me, yet he never spent the whole day with me, and tried to go on with his ordinary occupations. Our outward relations remained unchanged to the very day of our marriage: we went on saying 'you' and not 'thou' to each other; he did not even kiss my hand; he did not seek, but even avoided, opportunities of being alone with me. It was as if he feared to yield to the harmful excess of tenderness he felt. I don't know which of us had changed; but I now felt myself entirely his equal; I no longer found in him the pretence of simplicity which had displeased me earlier; and I often delighted to see in him, not a grown man inspiring respect and awe but a loving and wildly happy child. 'How mistaken I was about him!' I often thought; 'he is just such another human being as myself!' It seemed to me now, that his whole character was before me and that I thoroughly understood it. And how simple was every feature of his character, and how congenial to my own! Even his plans for our future life together were just my plans, only more clearly and better expressed in his words.

The weather was bad just then, and we spent most of our time indoors. The corner between the piano and the window was the scene of our best intimate talks. The candle-light was reflected on the blackness of the window near us; from time to time drops struck the glistening pane and rolled down. The rain pattered on the roof; the water splashed in a puddle under the spout; it felt damp near the window; but our corner seemed all the brighter and warmer and happier for that.

'Do you know, there is something I have long wished to say to you,' he began one night when we were sitting up late in our corner; 'I was thinking of it all the time you were playing.'

'Don't say it, I know all about it,' I replied.

'All right! mum's the word!'

'No! what is it?' I asked.

'Well, it is this. You remember the story I told you about A and B?'

'I should just think I did! What a stupid story! Lucky that it ended as it did!'

'Yes. I was very near destroying my happiness by my own act. You saved me. But the main thing is that I was always telling lies then, and I'm ashamed of it, and I want to have my say out now.'

'Please don't! you really mustn't!'

'Don't be frightened,' he said, smiling. 'I only want to justify myself. When I began then, I meant to argue.'

'It is always a mistake to argue,' I said.

'Yes, I argued wrong. After all my disappointments and mistakes in life, I told myself firmly when I came to the country this year, that love was no more for me, and that all I had to do was to grow old decently. So for a long time, I was unable to clear up my feeling towards you, or to make out where it might lead me. I hoped, and I didn't hope: at one time I thought you were trifling with me; at another I felt sure of you but could not decide what to do. But after that evening, you remember, when we walked in the garden at night, I got alarmed: the present happiness seemed too great to be real. What if I allowed myself to hope and then failed? But of course I was thinking only of myself, for I am disgustingly selfish.'

He stopped and looked at me.

'But it was not all nonsense that I said then. It was possible and right for me to have fears. I take so much from you and can give so little. You are still a child, a bud that has yet to open; you have never been in love before, and I . . .'

'Yes, do tell me the truth . . . ,' I began, and then stopped, afraid of his answer. 'No, never mind,' I added.

'Have I been in love before? is that it?' he said, guessing my thoughts at once. 'That I can tell you. No, never before—nothing at all like what I feel now.' But a sudden painful recollection seemed to flash across his mind. 'No,' he said sadly; 'in this too I need your compassion, in order to have the right to love you. Well, was I not bound to think twice before saying that I loved you? What do I give you? love, no doubt.'

'And is that little?' I asked, looking him in the face.

'Yes, my dear, it is little to give *you*,' he continued; 'you have youth and beauty. I often lie awake at night from happiness, and all the time I think of our future life together. I have lived through much, and now I think I have found what is needed for happiness. A quiet secluded life in the country, with the possibility of being useful to people to whom it is easy to do good, and who are not accustomed to have it done to them; then work which one hopes may be of some use; then rest, nature, books, music, love for one's neighbour—such is my idea of happiness.

And then, on the top of all that, you for a mate, and children, perhaps—what more can the heart of man desire?'

'It should be enough,' I said.

'Enough for me whose youth is over,' he went on, 'but not for you. Life is still before you, and you will perhaps seek happiness, and perhaps find it, in something different. You think now that this is happiness, because you love me.'

'You are wrong,' I said; 'I have always desired just that quiet domestic life and prized it. And you only say just what I have thought.'

He smiled.

'So you think, my dear; but that is not enough for you. You have youth and beauty,' he repeated thoughtfully.

But I was angry because he disbelieved me and seemed to cast my youth and beauty in my teeth.

'Why do you love me then?' I asked angrily; 'for my youth or for myself?'

'I don't know, but I love you,' he answered, looking at me with his attentive and attractive gaze.

I did not reply and involuntarily looked into his eyes. Suddenly a strange thing happened to me: first I ceased to see what was around me; then his face seemed to vanish till only the eyes were left, shining over against mine; next the eyes seemed to be in my own head, and then all became confused—I could see nothing and was forced to shut my eyes, in order to break loose from the feeling of pleasure and fear which his gaze was producing in me. . .

The day before our wedding-day, the weather cleared up towards evening. The rains which had begun in summer gave place to clear weather, and we had our first autumn evening, bright and cold. It was a wet, cold, shining world, and the garden showed for the first time the spaciousness and colour and bareness of autumn. The sky was clear, cold, and pale. I went to bed happy in the thought that to-morrow, our wedding-day, would be fine. I awoke with the sun, and the thought that this very day . . . seemed alarming and surprising. I went out into the garden. The sun had just risen and shone fitfully through the meager yellow leaves of the lime avenue. The path was strewn with rustling leaves, clusters of mountain-ash berries hung red and wrinkled on the boughs, with a sprinkling of frost-bitten crumpled leaves; the dahlias were black and wrinkled. The first rime lay like silver on the pale green of the grass and on the broken burdock plants round the house. In the clear cold sky there was not, and could not be, a single cloud.

'Can it possibly be to-day?' I asked myself, incredulous of my own happiness. 'Is it possible that I shall wake tomorrow, not here but in that strange house with the pillars? Is it possible that I shall never again wait for his coming and meet him, and sit up late with Kátya to talk about him? Shall I never sit with him beside the piano in our drawing-room? never see him off and feel uneasy about him on dark nights?' But I remembered that he promised yesterday to pay a last visit, and that Kátya had insisted on my trying on my wedding-dress, and had said 'For to-morrow'. I believed for a moment that it was all real, and then doubted again. 'Can it be that after to-day I shall be living there with a mother-in-law, without Nadëzha or old Grigóri or Kátya? Shall I go to bed without kissing my old nurse good-night and hearing her say, while she signs me with the cross from old custom, "Good-night, Miss"? Shall I never again teach Sónya and play with her and knock through the wall to her in the morning and hear her hearty laugh? Shall I become from to-day someone that I myself do not know? and is a new world, that will realize my hopes and desires, opening before me? and will that new world last for ever?' Alone with these thoughts I was depressed and impatient for his arrival. He came early, and it required his presence to convince me that I should really be his wife that very day, and the prospect ceased to frighten me.

Before dinner we walked to our church, to attend a memorial service for my father.

'If only he were living now!' I thought as we were returning and I leant silently on the arm of him who had been the dearest friend of the object of my thoughts. During the service, while I pressed my forehead against the cold stone of the chapel floor, I called up my father so vividly; I was so convinced that he understood me and approved my choice, that I felt as if his spirit were still hovering over us and blessing me. And my recollections and hopes, my joy and sadness, made up one solemn and satisfied feeling which was in harmony with the fresh still air, the silence, the bare fields and pale sky, from which the bright but powerless rays, trying in vain to burn my cheek, fell over all the landscape. My companion seemed to understand and share my feeling. He walked slowly and silently; and his face, at which I glanced from time to time, expressed the same serious mood between joy and sorrow which I shared with nature.

Suddenly he turned to me, and I saw that he intended to speak. 'Suppose he starts some other subject than that which is in my mind?' I thought. But he began to speak of my father and did not even name him.

'He once said to me in jest, "You should marry my Másha",' he began.

'He would have been happy now,' I answered, pressing closer the arm which held mine.

'You were a child then,' he went on, looking into my eyes; 'I loved those eyes then and used to kiss them only because they were like his, never thinking they would be so dear to me for their own sake. I used to call you Másha then.'

'I want you to say "thou" to me,' I said.

'I was just going to,' he answered; 'I feel for the first time that *thou art* entirely mine;' and his calm happy gaze that drew me to him rested on me.

We went on along the footpath over the beaten and trampled stubble; our voices and footsteps were the only sounds. On one side the brownish stubble stretched over a hollow to a distant leafless wood; across it at some distance a peasant was noiselessly ploughing a black strip which grew wider and wider. A drove of horses scattered under the hill seemed close to us. On the other side, as far as the garden and our house peeping through the trees, a field of winter corn, thawed by the sun, showed black with occasional patches of green. The winter sun shone over everything, and everything was covered with long gossamer spider's webs, which floated in the air round us, lay on the frost-dried stubble, and got into our eyes and hair and clothes. When we spoke, the sound of our voices hung in the motionless air above us, as if we two were alone in the whole world—alone under that azure vault, in which the beams of the winter sun played and flashed without scorching.

I too wished to say 'thou' to him, but I felt ashamed.

'Why *dost thou* walk so fast?' I said quickly and almost in a whisper; I could not help blushing.

He slackened his pace, and the gaze he turned on me was even more affectionate, gay, and happy.

At home we found that his mother and the inevitable guests had arrived already, and I was never alone with him again till we came out of church to drive to Nikólskoe.

The church was nearly empty: I just caught a glimpse of his mother standing up straight on a mat by the choir and of Kátya wearing a cap with purple ribbons and with tears on her cheeks, and of two or three of our servants looking curiously at me. I did not look at him, but felt his presence there beside me. I attended to the words of the prayers and repeated them, but they found no echo in my heart. Unable to pray, I looked listlessly at the icons, the candles, the embroidered cross on the priest's cope, the screen, and the window, and took nothing in. I only felt that something strange was being done to me. At last the priest turned to us with the cross in his hand, congratulated us, and said, 'I christened you and by God's mercy have lived to marry you.' Kátya and his mother kissed us, and Grigóri's voice was heard, calling up the carriage. But I was only frightened and disappointed: all was over, but nothing extraordinary, nothing worthy of the Sacrament I had just received, had taken place in myself. He and I exchanged kisses, but the kiss seemed strange and not expressive of our feeling. 'Is this all?' I thought. We went out of church, the sound of wheels reverberated under the vaulted roof, the fresh air blew on my face, he put on his hat and handed me into the carriage. Through the window I could see a frosty moon with a halo round it. He sat down beside me and shut the door after him. I felt a sudden pang. The assurance of his proceedings seemed to me insulting. Kátya called out that I should put something on my head; the wheels rumbled on the stone and then moved along the soft road, and we were off. Huddling in a corner, I looked out at the distant fields and the road flying past in the cold glitter of the moon. Without looking at him, I felt his presence beside me. 'Is this all I have got from the moment, of which I expected so much?' I thought; and still it seemed humiliating and insulting to be sitting alone with him, and so close. I turned to him, intending to speak; but the words would not come, as if my love had vanished, giving place to a feeling of mortification and alarm.

'Till this moment I did not believe it was possible,' he said in a low voice in answer to my look.

'But I am afraid somehow,' I said.

'Afraid of me, my dear?' he said, taking my hand and bending over it.

My hand lay lifeless in his, and the cold at my heart was painful.

'Yes,' I whispered.

But at that moment my heart began to beat faster, my hand trembled and pressed his, I grew hot, my eyes sought his in the half-darkness, and all at once I felt that I did not fear him, that this fear was love—a new love still more tender and stronger than the old. I felt that I was wholly his, and that I was happy in his power over me.

Part II

I

Days, weeks, two whole months of seclusion in the country slipped by unnoticed, as we thought then; and yet those two months comprised feelings, emotions, and happiness, sufficient for a lifetime. Our plans for the regulation of our life in the country were not carried out at all in the way that we expected; but the reality was not inferior to our ideal. There was none of that hard work, performance of duty, self-sacrifice, and life for others, which I had pictured to myself before our marriage; there was, on the contrary, merely a selfish feeling of love for one another, a wish to be loved, a constant causeless gaiety and entire oblivion of all the world. It is true that my husband some-times went to his study to work, or drove to town on business, or walked about attending to the management of the estate; but I saw what it cost him to tear himself away from me. He confessed later that every occupation, in my absence, seemed to him mere nonsense in which it was impossible to take any interest. It was just the same with me. If I read, or played the piano, or passed my time with his mother, or taught in the school, I did so only because each of these occupations was connected with him and won his approval; but whenever the thought of him was not associated with any duty, my hands fell by my sides and it seemed to me absurd to think that anything existed apart from him. Perhaps it was a wrong and selfish feel-ing, but it gave me happiness and lifted me high above all the world. He alone existed on earth for me, and I considered him the best and most faultless man in the world; so that I could not live for anything else than for him, and my one object was to realize his conception of me. And in his eyes I was the first and most excellent woman in the world, the possessor of all possible virtues; and I strove to be that woman in the opinion of the first and best of men.

He came to my room one day while I was praying. I looked round at him and went on with my prayers. Not wishing to interrupt me, he sat down at a table and opened a book. But I thought he was looking at me and looked round myself. He smiled, I laughed, and had to stop my prayers.

'Have you prayed already?' I asked.

'Yes. But you go on; I'll go away.'

'You do say your prayers, I hope?'

He made no answer and was about to leave the room when I stopped him.

'Darling, for my sake, please repeat the prayers with me!' He stood up beside me, dropped his arms awkwardly, and began, with a serious face and some hesitation. Occasionally he turned towards me, seeking signs of approval and aid in my face.

When he came to an end, I laughed and embraced him.

'I feel just as if I were ten! And you do it all!' he said, blushing and kissing my hands.

Our house was one of those old-fashioned country houses in which several generations have passed their lives together under one roof, respecting and loving one another. It was all redolent of good sound family traditions, which as soon as I entered it seemed to become mine too. The management of the household was carried on by Tatyána Semënovna, my mother-in-law, on old-fashioned lines. Of grace and beauty there was not much; but, from the servants down to the furniture and food, there

was abundance of everything, and a general cleanliness, solid-
ity, and order, which inspired respect. The drawing-room furniture was arranged symmetrically; there were portraits on the
walls, and the floor was covered with home-made carpets and
mats. In the morning-room there was an old piano, with chif-
foniers of two different patterns, sofas, and little carved tables
with bronze ornaments. My sitting-room, specially arranged by
Tatyána Semënovna, contained the best furniture in the house,
of many styles and periods, including an old pierglass, which I
was frightened to look into at first, but came to value as an old
friend. Though Tatyána Semënovna's voice was never heard,
the whole household went like a clock. The number of servants
was far too large (they all wore soft boots with no heels, because
Tatyána Semënovna had an intense dislike for stamping heels
and creaking soles); but they all seemed proud of their calling,
trembled before their old mistress, treated my husband and me
with an affectionate air of patronage, and performed their du-
ties, to all appearance, with extreme satisfaction. Every Saturday the floors were scoured and the carpets beaten without fail;
on the first of every month there was a religious service in the
house and holy water was sprinkled; on Tatyána Semënovna's
name-day and on her son's (and on mine too, beginning from
that autumn) an entertainment was regularly provided for
the whole neighbourhood. And all this had gone on without a
break ever since the beginning of Tatyána Semënovna's life.

My husband took no part in the household management,
he attended only to the farm-work and the labourers, and gave
much time to this. Even in winter he got up so early that I often woke to find him gone. He generally came back for early
tea, which we drank alone together; and at that time, when the

worries and vexations of the farm were over, he was almost always in that state of high spirits which we called 'wild ecstasy'. I often made him tell me what he had been doing in the morning, and he gave such absurd accounts that we both laughed till we cried. Sometimes I insisted on a serious account, and he gave it, restraining a smile. I watched his eyes and moving lips and took nothing in: the sight of him and the sound of his voice was pleasure enough.

'Well, what have I been saying? repeat it,' he would sometimes say. But I could repeat nothing. It seemed so absurd that *he* should talk to *me* of any other subject than ourselves. As if it mattered in the least what went on in the world outside! It was at a much later time that I began to some extent to understand and take an interest in his occupations. Tatyána Semënovna never appeared before dinner: she breakfasted alone and said good-morning to us by deputy. In our exclusive little world of frantic happiness a voice from the staid orderly region in which she dwelt was quite startling: I often lost self-control and could only laugh without speaking, when the maid stood before me with folded hands and made her formal report: 'The mistress bade me inquire how you slept after your walk yesterday evening; and about her I was to report that she had pain in her side all night, and a stupid dog barked in the village and kept her awake: and also I was to ask how you liked the bread this morning, and to tell you that it was not Tarás who baked to-day, but Nikoláshka who was trying his hand for the first time; and she says his baking is not at all bad, especially the cracknels: but the tea-rusks were over-baked.' Before dinner we saw little of each other: he wrote or went out again while I played the piano or read; but at four o'clock we all met in the drawing-room before dinner. Tatyána Semënovna sailed out of her own room, and certain poor and pious maiden ladies, of whom there were always two or three living in the house, made their appearance also. Every day without fail my husband by old habit offered his arm to his mother, to take her in to dinner; but she insisted that I should take the other, so that every day, without fail, we stuck in the doors and got in each other's way. She also presided at dinner, where the conversation, if rather solemn, was polite and sensible. The commonplace talk between my husband and me was a pleasant interruption to the formality of those entertainments. Sometimes there were squabbles between mother and son and they bantered one another; and I especially enjoyed those scenes, because they were the best proof of the strong and tender love which united the two. After dinner Tatyána Semënovna went to the parlour, where she sat in an armchair and ground her snuff or cut the leaves of new books, while we read aloud or went off to the piano in the morning-room. We read much together at this time, but music was our favourite and best enjoyment, always evoking fresh chords in our hearts and as it were revealing each afresh to the other. While I played his favourite pieces, he sat on a distant sofa where I could hardly see him. He was ashamed to betray the impression produced on him by the music; but often, when he was not expecting it, I rose from the piano, went up to him, and tried to detect on his face signs of emotion—the unnatural brightness and moistness of the eyes, which he tried in vain to conceal. Tatyána Semënovna, though she often wanted to take a look at us there, was also anxious to put no constraint upon us. So she always passed through the room with an air of indifference and a pretence of being busy; but I knew that she had no real reason for going to her room and returning so soon. In the evening I poured out tea in the large drawing-room, and all the household met again. This solemn ceremony of distributing cups and glasses before the solemnly shining samovar made me nervous for a long time. I felt myself still unworthy of such a distinction, too young and frivolous to turn the tap of such a big samovar, to put glasses on Nikíta's salver, saying 'For Peter Ivánovich', 'For Márya Mínichna', to ask 'Is it sweet enough?' and to leave out lumps of sugar for Nurse and other deserving persons. 'Capital! Capital! Just like a grown-up person!' was a frequent comment from my husband, which only increased my confusion.

After tea Tatyána Semënovna played patience or listened to Márya Mínichna telling fortunes by the cards. Then she kissed us both and signed us with the cross, and we went off to our own rooms. But we generally sat up together till midnight, and that was our best and pleasantest time. He told me stories of his past life; we made plans and sometimes even talked philosophy; but we tried always to speak low, for fear we should be heard upstairs and reported to Tatyána Semënovna, who insisted on our going to bed early. Sometimes we grew hungry; and then we stole off to the pantry, secured a cold supper by the good offices of Nikíta, and ate it in my sitting-room by the light of one candle. He and I lived like strangers in that big old house, where the uncompromising spirit of the past and of Tatyána Semënovna ruled supreme. Not she only, but the servants, the old ladies, the furniture, even the pictures, inspired me with respect and a little alarm, and made me feel that he and I were a little out of place in that house and must always be very careful and cautious in our doings. Thinking it over now, I see that many things—the pressure of that unvarying routine, and that crowd of idle and inquisitive servants—were uncomfortable and oppressive; but at the time that very constraint made our love for one another still keener. Not I only, but he also, never grumbled openly at anything; on the contrary he shut his eyes to what was amiss. Dmítri Sídorov, one of the footmen, was a great smoker; and regularly every day, when we two were in the morning-room after dinner, he went to my husband's study to take tobacco from the jar; and it was a sight to see Sergéy Mikháylych creeping on tiptoe to me with a face between delight and terror, and a wink and a warning forefinger, while he pointed at Dmítri Sídorov, who was quite unconscious of being watched. Then, when Dmítri Sídorov had gone away without having seen us, in his joy that all had passed off successfully, he declared (as he did on every other occasion) that I was a darling, and kissed me. At times his calm connivance and apparent indifference to everything annoyed me, and I took it for weakness, never noticing that I acted in the same way myself. 'It's like a child who dares not show his will,' I thought.

'My dear! my dear!' he said once when I told him that his weakness surprised me; 'how can a man, as happy as I am, be dissatisfied with anything? Better to give way myself than to put compulsion on others; of that I have long been convinced. There is no condition in which one cannot be happy; but our life is such bliss! I simply cannot be angry; to me now nothing seems bad, but only pitiful and amusing. Above all—*le mieux est l'ennemi du bien.* Will you believe it, when I hear a ring at the bell, or receive a letter, or even wake up in the morning, I'm frightened. Life must go on, something may change; and nothing can be better than the present.'

I believed him but did not understand him. I was happy; but I took that as a matter of course, the invariable experience of people in our position, and believed that there was somewhere, I knew not where, a different happiness, not greater but different.

So two months went by and winter came with its cold and snow; and, in spite of his company, I began to feel lonely, that life was repeating itself, that there was nothing new either in him or in myself, and that we were merely going back to what had been before. He began to give more time to business which kept him away from me, and my old feeling returned, that there was a special department of his mind into which he was unwilling to admit me. His unbroken calmness provoked me. I loved him as much as ever and was as happy as ever in his love; but my love, instead of increasing, stood still; and another new and disquieting sensation began to creep into my heart. To love him was not enough for me after the happiness I had felt in falling in love. I wanted movement and not a calm course of existence. I wanted excitement and danger and the chance to sacrifice myself for my love. I felt in myself a superabundance of energy which found no outlet in our quiet life. I had fits of depression which I was ashamed of and tried to conceal from him, and fits of excessive tenderness and high spirits which alarmed him. He realized my state of mind before I did, and proposed a visit to Petersburg; but I begged him to give this up and not to change our manner of life or spoil our happiness. Happy indeed I was; but I was tormented by the thought that this happiness cost me no effort and no sacrifice, though I was even painfully conscious of my power to face both. I loved him and saw that I was all in all to him; but I wanted everyone to see our love; I wanted to love him in spite of obstacles. My mind, and even my senses, were fully occupied; but there was another feeling of youth and craving for movement, which found no satisfaction in our quiet life. What made him say that, whenever I liked, we could go to town? Had he not said so I might have realized that my uncomfortable feelings were my own fault and dangerous nonsense, and that the sacrifice I desired was there before me, in the task of overcoming these feelings. I was haunted by the thought that I could escape from depression by a mere change from the country; and at the same time I felt ashamed and sorry to tear him away, out of selfish motives, from all he cared for. So time went on, the snow grew deeper, and there we remained together, all alone and just the same as before, while outside I knew there was noise and glitter and excitement, and hosts of people suffering or rejoicing without one thought of us and our remote existence. I suffered most from the feeling that custom was daily petrifying our lives into one fixed shape, that our minds were losing their freedom and becoming enslaved to the steady passionless course of time. The morning always found us cheerful; we were polite at dinner, and affectionate in the evening. 'It is all right,' I thought, 'to do good to others and lead upright lives, as he says; but there is time for that later; and there are other things, for which the time is now or never.' I wanted, not what I had got, but a life of struggle; I wanted feeling to be the guide of life, and not life to guide feeling. If only I could go with him to the edge of a precipice and say, 'One step, and I shall fall over—one movement, and I shall be lost!' Then, pale with fear, he would catch me in his strong arms and hold me over the edge till my blood froze, and then carry me off whither he pleased.

This state of feeling even affected my health, and I began to suffer from nerves. One morning I was worse than usual. He had come back from the estate-office out of sorts, which was a rare thing with him. I noticed it at once and asked what was the matter. He would not tell me and said it was of no importance. I found out afterwards that the police-inspector, out of spite against my husband, was summoning our peasants, making illegal demands on them, and using threats to them. My husband could not swallow this at once; he could not feel it merely 'pitiful and amusing'. He was provoked, and therefore unwilling to speak of it to me. But it seemed to me that he did not wish to speak to me about it because he considered me a mere child, incapable of understanding his concerns. I turned from him and said no more. I then told the servant to ask Márya Mínichna, who was staying in the house, to join us at breakfast. I ate my breakfast very fast and took her to the morning-room, where I began to talk loudly to her about some trifle which did not interest me in the least. He walked about the room, glancing at us from time to time. This made me more and more inclined to talk and even to laugh; all that I said myself, and all that Márya Mínichna said, seemed to me laughable. Without a word to me he went off to his study and shut the door behind him. When I ceased to hear him, all my high spirits vanished at once: indeed Márya Mínichna was surprised and asked what was the matter. I sat down on a sofa without answering, and felt ready to cry. 'What has he got on his mind?' I wondered; 'some trifle which he thinks important; but, if he tried to tell it me, I should soon show him it was mere nonsense. But he must needs think that I won't understand, must humiliate me by his majestic composure, and always be in the right as against me. But I too am in the right when I find things tiresome and trivial,' I reflected; 'and I do well to want an active life rather than to stagnate in one spot and feel life flowing past me. I want to move forward, to have some new experience every day and every hour, whereas he wants to stand still and to keep me standing beside him. And how easy it would be for him to gratify me! He need not take me to town; he need only be like me and not put compulsion on himself and regulate his feelings, but live simply. That is the advice he gives me, but he is not simple himself. That is what is the matter.'

I felt the tears rising and knew that I was irritated with him. My irritation frightened me, and I went to his study. He was sitting at the table, writing. Hearing my step, he looked up for a moment and then went on writing; he seemed calm and unconcerned. His look vexed me: instead of going up to him, I stood beside his writing-table, opened a book, and began to look at it. He broke off his writing again and looked at me.

'Másha, are you out of sorts?' he asked.

I replied with a cold look, as much as to say, 'You are very polite, but what is the use of asking?' He shook his head and smiled with a tender timid air; but his smile, for the first time, drew no answering smile from me.

'What happened to you to-day?' I asked; 'why did you not tell me?'

'Nothing much—a trifling nuisance,' he said. 'But I might tell you now. Two of our serfs went off to the town . . .'

But I would not let him go on.

'Why would you not tell me, when I asked you at breakfast?'

'I was angry then and should have said something foolish.'

'I wished to know then.'

'Why?'

'Why do you suppose that I can never help you in anything?'

'Not help me!' he said, dropping his pen. 'Why, I believe that without you I could not live. You not only help me in everything I do, but you do it yourself. You are very wide of the mark,' he said, and laughed. 'My life depends on you. I am pleased with things, only because you are there, because I need you . . .'

'Yes, I know; I am a delightful child who must be humoured and kept quiet,' I said in a voice that astonished him, so that he looked up as if this was a new experience; 'but I don't want to be quiet and calm; that is more in your line, and too much in your line,' I added.

'Well,' he began quickly, interrupting me and evidently afraid to let me continue, 'when I tell you the facts, I should like to know your opinion.'

'I don't want to hear them now,' I answered. I did want to hear the story, but I found it so pleasant to break down his composure. 'I don't want to play at life,' I said, 'but to live, as you do yourself.'

His face, which reflected every feeling so quickly and so vividly, now expressed pain and intense attention.

'I want to share your life, to . . . ,' but I could not go on—his face showed such deep distress. He was silent for a moment.

'But what part of my life do you not share?' he asked; 'is it because I, and not you, have to bother with the inspector and with tipsy labourers?'

'That's not the only thing,' I said.

'For God's sake try to understand me, my dear!' he cried. 'I know that excitement is always painful; I have learnt that from the experience of life. I love you, and I can't but wish to save you from excitement. My life consists of my love for you; so you should not make life impossible for me.'

'You are always in the right,' I said without looking at him.

I was vexed again by his calmness and coolness while I was conscious of annoyance and some feeling akin to penitence.

'Másha, what is the matter?' he asked. 'The question is not, which of us is in the right— not at all; but rather, what grievance have you against me? Take time before you answer, and tell me all that is in your mind. You are dissatisfied with me: and you are, no doubt, right; but let me understand what I have done wrong.'

But how could I put my feeling into words? That he understood me at once, that I again stood before him like a child, that I could do nothing without his understanding and foreseeing it—all this only increased my agitation.

'I have no complaint to make of you,' I said; 'I am merely bored and want not to be bored. But you say that it can't be helped, and, as always, you are right.'

I looked at him as I spoke. I had gained my object: his calmness had disappeared, and I read fear and pain in his face.

'Másha,' he began in a low troubled voice, 'this is no mere trifle: the happiness of our lives is at stake. Please hear me out without answering. Why do you wish to torment me?'

But I interrupted him.

'Oh, I know you will turn out to be right. Words are useless; of course you are right.' I spoke coldly, as if some evil spirit were speaking with my voice.

'If you only knew what you are doing!' he said, and his voice shook.

I burst out crying and felt relieved. He sat down beside me and said nothing. I felt sorry for him, ashamed of myself, and annoyed at what I had done. I avoided looking at him. I felt that any look from him at that moment must express severity or perplexity. At last I looked up and saw his eyes: they were fixed on me with a tender gentle expression that seemed to ask for pardon. I caught his hand and said, 'Forgive me! I don't know myself what I have been saying.'

'But I do; and you spoke the truth.'

'What do you mean?' I asked.

'That we must go to Petersburg,' he said; 'there is nothing for us to do here just now.'

'As you please,' I said.

He took me in his arms and kissed me.

'You must forgive me,' he said; 'for I am to blame.'

That evening I played to him for a long time, while he walked about the room. He had a habit of muttering to himself; and when I asked him what he was muttering, he always thought for a moment and then told me exactly what it was. It was generally verse, and sometimes mere nonsense, but I could always judge of his mood by it. When I asked him now, he stood still, thought an instant, and then repeated two lines from Lérmontov:

> He in his madness prays for storms,
> And dreams that storms will bring him peace.

'He is really more than human,' I thought; 'he knows everything. How can one help loving him?'

I got up, took his arm, and began to walk up and down with him, trying to keep step.

'Well?' he asked, smiling and looking at me.

'All right,' I whispered. And then a sudden fit of merriment came over us both: our eyes laughed, we took longer and longer steps, and rose higher and higher on tiptoe. Prancing in this manner, to the profound dissatisfaction of the butler and astonishment of my mother-in-law, who was playing patience in the parlour, we proceeded through the house till we reached the dining-room; there we stopped, looked at one another, and burst out laughing.

A fortnight later, before Christmas, we were in Petersburg.

II

The journey to Petersburg, a week in Moscow, visits to my own relations and my husband's, settling down in our new quarters, travel, new towns and new faces—all this passed before me like a dream. It was all so new, various, and delightful, so warmly and brightly lighted up by his presence and his love, that our quiet life in the country seemed to me something very remote and unimportant. I had expected to find people in society proud and cold; but to my great surprise, I was received everywhere with unfeigned cordiality and pleasure, not only by relations, but also by strangers. I seemed to be the one object of their thoughts, and my arrival the one thing they wanted, to complete their happiness. I was surprised too to discover in what seemed to me the very best society a number of people acquainted with my husband, though he had never spoken of them to me; and I often felt it odd and disagreeable to hear him now speak disapprovingly of some of these people who seemed to me so kind. I could not understand his coolness towards them or his endeavours to avoid many acquaintances that seemed to me flattering. Surely, the more kind people one knows, the better; and here everyone was kind.

'This is how we must manage, you see,' he said to me before we left the country; 'here we are little Croesuses, but in town we shall not be at all rich. So we must not stay after Easter, or go into society, or we shall get into difficulties. For your sake too I should not wish it.'

'Why should we go into society?' I asked; 'we shall have a look at the theatres, see our relations, go to the opera, hear some good music, and be ready to come home before Easter.'

But these plans were forgotten the moment we got to Petersburg. I found myself at once in such a new and delightful world, surrounded by so many pleasures and confronted by such novel interests, that I instantly, though unconsciously, turned my back on my past life and its plans. 'All that was preparatory, a mere playing at life; but here is the real thing! And there is the future too!' Such were my thoughts. The restlessness and symptoms of depression which had troubled me at home vanished at once and entirely, as if by magic. My love for my husband grew calmer, and I ceased to wonder whether he loved me less. Indeed I could not doubt his love: every thought of mine was understood at once, every feeling shared, and every wish gratified by him. His composure, if it still existed, no longer provoked me. I also began to realize that he not only loved me but was proud of me. If we paid a call, or made some new acquaintance, or gave an evening party at which I, trembling inwardly from fear of disgracing myself, acted as hostess, he often said when it was over: 'Bravo, young woman! capital! you needn't be frightened; a real success!' And his praise gave me great pleasure. Soon after our arrival he wrote to his mother and asked me to add a post-script, but refused to let me see his letter; of course I insisted on reading it; and he had said: 'You would not know Másha again, I don't myself. Where does she get that charming graceful self-confidence and ease, such social gifts with such simplicity and charm and kindliness? Everybody is delighted with her. I can't admire her enough myself, and should be more in love with her than ever, if that were possible.'

'Now I know what I am like,' I thought. In my joy and pride I felt that I loved him more than before. My success with all our new acquaintances was a complete surprise to me. I heard on all sides, how this uncle had taken a special fancy for me, and that aunt was raving about me; I was told by one admirer that I had no rival among the Petersburg ladies, and assured by another, a lady, that I might, if I cared, lead the fashion in society. A cousin of my husband's, in particular, a Princess D., middle-aged and very much at home in society, fell in love with me at first sight and paid me compliments which turned my head. The first time that she invited me to a ball and spoke to my husband about it, he turned to me and asked if I wished to go; I could just detect a sly smile on his face. I nodded assent and felt that I was blushing.

'She looks like a criminal when confessing what she wishes,' he said with a good-natured laugh.

'But you said that we must not go into society, and you don't care for it yourself,' I answered, smiling and looking implor-ingly at him.

'Let us go, if you want to very much,' he said.

'Really, we had better not.'

'Do you want to? very badly?' he asked again.

I said nothing.

'Society in itself is no great harm,' he went on; 'but unsatisfied social aspirations are a bad and ugly business. We must certainly accept, and we will.'

'To tell you the truth,' I said, "I never in my life longed for anything as much as I do for this ball.'

So we went, and my delight exceeded all my expectations. It seemed to me, more than ever, that I was the centre round which everything revolved, that for my sake alone this great room was lighted up and the band played, and that this crowd of people had assembled to admire me. From the hairdresser and the lady's maid to my partners and the old gentlemen promenading the ball-room, all alike seemed to make it plain that they were in love with me. The general verdict formed at the ball about me and reported by my cousin, came to this: I was quite unlike the other women and had a rural simplicity and charm of my own. I was so flattered by my success that I frankly told my husband I should like to attend two or three more balls during the season, and 'so get thoroughly sick of them', I added; but I did not mean what I said.

He agreed readily; and he went with me at first with obvious satisfaction. He took pleasure in my success, and seemed to have quite forgotten his former warning or to have changed his opinion.

But a time came when he was evidently bored and wearied by the life we were leading. I was too busy, however, to think about that. Even if I sometimes noticed his eyes fixed questioningly on me with a serious attentive gaze, I did not realize its meaning. I was utterly blinded by this sudden affection which I seemed to evoke in all our new acquaintances, and confused by the unfamiliar atmosphere of luxury, refinement, and novelty. It pleased me so much to find myself in these surroundings not merely his equal but his superior, and yet to love him better and more independently than before, that I could not understand what he could object to for me in society life. I had a new sense of pride and self-satisfaction when my entry at a ball attracted all eyes, while he, as if ashamed to confess his ownership of me in public, made haste to leave my side and efface himself in the crowd of black coats. 'Wait a little!' I often said in my heart, when I identified his obscure and sometimes woebegone figure at the end of the room—'Wait till we get home! Then you will see and understand for whose sake I try to be beautiful and brilliant, and what it is I love in all that surrounds me this evening!' I really believed that my success pleased me only because it enabled me to give it up for his sake. One danger I recognized as possible—that I might be carried away by a fancy for some new acquaintance, and that my husband might grow jealous. But he trusted me so absolutely, and seemed so undisturbed and indifferent, and all the young men were so inferior to him, that I was not alarmed by this one danger. Yet the attention of so many people in society gave me satisfaction, flattered my vanity, and made me think that there was some merit in my love for my husband. Thus I became more offhand and self-confident in my behaviour to him.

'Oh, I saw you this evening carrying on a most animated conversation with Mme N.,' I said one night on returning from a ball, shaking my finger at him. He had really been talking to this lady, who was a well-known figure in Petersburg society. He was more silent and depressed than usual, and I said this to rouse him up.

'What is the good of talking like that, for *you* especially, Másha?' he said with half-closed teeth and frowning as if in pain. 'Leave that to others; it does not suit you and me. Pretence of that sort may spoil the true relation between us, which I still hope may come back.'

I was ashamed and said nothing.

'Will it ever come back, Másha, do you think?' he asked.

'It never was spoilt and never will be,' I said; and I really believed this then.

'God grant that you are right!' he said; 'if not, we ought to be going home.'

But he only spoke like this once—in general he seemed as satisfied as I was, and I was so gay and so happy! I comforted myself too by thinking, 'If he is bored sometimes, I endured the same thing for his sake in the country. If the relation between us has become a little different, everything will be the same again in summer, when we shall be alone in our house at Nikólskoe with Tatyána Semënovna.'

So the winter slipped by, and we stayed on, in spite of our plans, over Easter in Petersburg. A week later we were preparing to start; our packing was all done; my husband, who had bought things—plants for the garden and presents for people at Nikólskoe, was in a specially cheerful and affectionate mood. Just then Princess D. came and begged us to stay till the Saturday, in order to be present at a reception to be given by Countess R. The Countess was very anxious to secure me, because a foreign prince, who was visiting Petersburg and had seen me already at a ball, wished to make my acquaintance; indeed this was his motive for attending the reception, and he declared that I was the most beautiful woman in Russia. All the world was to be there; and, in a word, it would really be too bad, if I did not go too.

My husband was talking to someone at the other end of the drawing-room.

'So you will go, won't you, Mary?' said the Princess.

'We meant to start for the country the day after tomorrow,' I answered undecidedly, glancing at my husband. Our eyes met, and he turned away at once.

'I must persuade him to stay,' she said, 'and then we can go on Saturday and turn all heads. All right?'

'It would upset our plans; and we have packed,' I answered, beginning to give way.

'She had better go this evening and make her curtsey to the Prince,' my husband called out from the other end of the room; and he spoke in a tone of suppressed irritation which I had never heard from him before.

'I declare he's jealous, for the first time in his life,' said the lady, laughing. 'But it's not for the sake of the Prince I urge it, Sergéy Mikháylych, but for all our sakes. The Countess was so anxious to have her.'

'It rests with her entirely,' my husband said coldly, and then left the room.

I saw that he was much disturbed, and this pained me. I gave no positive promise. As soon as our visitor left, I went to my husband. He was walking up and down his room, thinking, and neither saw nor heard me when I came in on tiptoe.

Looking at him I said to myself: 'He is dreaming already of his dear Nikólskoe, our morning coffee in the bright drawing-room, the land and the labourers, our evenings in the music-room, and our secret midnight suppers.' Then I decided in my own heart: 'Not for all the balls and all the flattering princes in the world will I give up his glad confusion and tender cares.' I was just about to say that I did not wish to go to the ball and would refuse, when he looked round, saw me, and frowned. His face, which had been gentle and thoughtful, changed at once to its old expression of sagacity, penetration, and patronizing composure. He would not show himself to me as a mere man, but had to be a demigod on a pedestal.

'Well, my dear?' he asked, turning towards me with an unconcerned air.

I said nothing. I was provoked, because he was hiding his real self from me, and would not continue to be the man I loved.

'Do you want to go to this reception on Saturday?' he asked.

'I did, but you disapprove. Besides, our things are all packed,' I said.

Never before had I heard such coldness in his tone to me, and never before seen such coldness in his eye.

'I shall order the things to be unpacked,' he said, 'and I shall stay till Tuesday. So you can go to the party, if you like. I hope you will; but I shall not go.'

Without looking at me, he began to walk about the room jerkily, as his habit was when perturbed.

'I simply can't understand you,' I said, following him with my eyes from where I stood. 'You say that you never lose self-control' (he had never really said so); 'then why do you talk to me so strangely? I am ready on your account to sacrifice this pleasure, and then you, in a sarcastic tone which is new from you to me, insist that I should go.'

'So you make a *sacrifice*!' he threw special emphasis on the last word. 'Well, so do I. What could be better? We compete in generosity—what an example of family happiness!'

Such harsh and contemptuous language I had never heard from his lips before. I was not abashed, but mortified by his contempt; and his harshness did not frighten me but made me harsh too. How could *he* speak thus, he who was always so frank and simple and dreaded insincerity in our speech to one another? And what had I done that he should speak so? I really intended to sacrifice for his sake a pleasure in which I could see no harm; and a moment ago I loved him and understood his feelings as well as ever. We had changed parts: now he avoided direct and plain words, and I desired them.

'You are much changed,' I said, with a sigh. 'How am I guilty before you? It is not this party—you have something else, some old count against me. Why this insincerity? You used to be so afraid of it yourself. Tell me plainly what you complain of.' 'What will he say?' thought I, and reflected with some complacency that I had done nothing all winter which he could find fault with.

I went into the middle of the room, so that he had to pass close to me, and looked at him. I thought, 'He will come and clasp me in his arms, and there will be an end of it.' I was even sorry that I should not have the chance of proving him wrong. But he stopped at the far end of the room and looked at me.

'Do you not understand yet?' he asked.

'No, I don't.'

'Then I must explain. What I feel, and cannot help feeling, positively sickens me for the first time in my life.' He stopped, evidently startled by the harsh sound of his own voice.

'What do you mean?' I asked, with tears of indignation in my eyes.

'It sickens me that the Prince admired you, and you therefore run to meet him, forgetting your husband and yourself and womanly dignity; and you wilfully misunderstand what your want of self-respect makes your husband feel for you: you actually come to your husband and speak of the "sacrifice" you are making, by which you mean—"To show myself to His Highness is a great pleasure to me, but I 'sacrifice' it." '

The longer he spoke, the more he was excited by the sound of his own voice, which was hard and rough and cruel. I had never seen him, had never thought of seeing him, like that. The blood rushed to my heart and I was frightened; but I felt that I had nothing to be ashamed of, and the excitement of wounded vanity made me eager to punish him.

'I have long been expecting this,' I said. 'Go on. Go on!'

'What you expected, I don't know,' he went on; 'but I might well expect the worst, when I saw you day after day sharing the dirtiness and idleness and luxury of this foolish society, and it has come at last. Never have I felt such shame and pain as now—pain for myself, when your friend thrusts her unclean fingers into my heart and speaks of my jealousy!—jealousy of a man whom neither you nor I know; and you refuse to understand me and offer to make a sacrifice for me—and what sacrifice? I am ashamed for you, for your degradation! . . . Sacrifice!' he repeated again.

'Ah, so this is a husband's power,' thought I: 'to insult and humiliate a perfectly innocent woman. Such may be a husband's rights, but I will not submit to them.' I felt the blood leave my face and a strange distension of my nostrils, as I said,

'No! I make no sacrifice on your account. I shall go to the party on Saturday without fail.'

'And I hope you may enjoy it. But all is over between us two!' he cried out in a fit of unrestrained fury. 'But you shall not torture me any longer! I was a fool, when I . . .', but his lips quivered, and he refrained with a visible effort from ending the sentence.

I feared and hated him at that moment. I wished to say a great deal to him and punish him for all his insults; but if I had opened my mouth, I should have lost my dignity by bursting into tears. I said nothing and left the room. But as soon as I ceased to hear his footsteps, I was horrified at what we had done. I feared that the tie which had made all my happiness might really be snapped for ever; and I thought of going back. But then I wondered: 'Is he calm enough now to understand me, if I mutely stretch out my hand and look at him? Will he realize my generosity? What if he calls my grief a mere pretence? Or he may feel sure that he is right and accept my repentance and forgive me with unruffled pride. And why, oh why, did he whom I loved so well insult me so cruelly?'

I went not to him but to my own room, where I sat for a long time and cried. I recalled with horror each word of our conversation, and substituted different words, kind words, for those that we had spoken, and added others; and then again I remembered the reality with horror and a feeling of injury. In the evening I went down for tea and met my husband in the presence of a friend who was staying with us; and it seemed to me that a wide gulf had opened between us from that day. Our friend asked me when we were to start; and before I could speak, my husband answered:

'On Tuesday,' he said; 'we have to stay for Countess R.'s reception.' He turned to me: 'I believe you intend to go?' he asked.

His matter-of-fact tone frightened me, and I looked at him timidly. His eyes were directed straight at me with an unkind and scornful expression; his voice was cold and even.

'Yes,' I answered.

When we were alone that evening, he came up to me and held out his hand.

'Please forget what I said to you to-day,' he began.

As I took his hand, a smile quivered on my lips and the tears were ready to flow; but he took his hand away and sat down on an armchair at some distance, as if fearing a sentimental scene. 'Is it possible that he still thinks himself in the right?' I wondered; and, though I was quite ready to explain and to beg that we might not go to the party, the words died on my lips.

'I must write to my mother that we have put off our departure,' he said; 'otherwise she will be uneasy.'

'When do you think of going?' I asked.

'On Tuesday, after the reception,' he replied.

'I hope it is not on my account,' I said, looking into his eyes; but those eyes merely looked—they said nothing, and a veil seemed to cover them from me. His face seemed to me to have grown suddenly old and disagreeable.

We went to the reception, and good friendly relations between us seemed to have been restored, but these relations were quite different from what they had been.

At the party I was sitting with other ladies when the Prince came up to me, so that I had to stand up in order to speak to him. As I rose, my eyes involuntarily sought my husband. He was looking at me from the other end of the room, and now turned away. I was seized by a sudden sense of shame and pain; in my confusion I blushed all over my face and neck under the Prince's eye. But I was forced to stand and listen, while he spoke, eyeing me from his superior height. Our conversation was soon over: there was no room for him beside me, and he, no doubt, felt that I was uncomfortable with him. We talked of the last ball, of where I should spend the summer, and so on. As he left me, he expressed a wish to make the acquaintance of my husband, and I saw them meet and begin a conversation at the far end of the room. The Prince evidently said something about me; for he smiled in the middle of their talk and looked in my direction.

My husband suddenly flushed up. He made a low bow and turned away from the Prince without being dismissed. I blushed too: I was ashamed of the impression which I and, still more, my husband must have made on the Prince. Everyone, I thought, must have noticed my awkward shyness when I was presented, and my husband's eccentric behaviour. 'Heaven knows how they will interpret such conduct? Perhaps they know already about my scene with my husband!'

Princess D. drove me home, and on the way I spoke to her about my husband. My patience was at an end, and I told her the whole story of what had taken place between us owing to this unlucky party. To calm me, she said that such differences were very common and quite unimportant, and that our quarrel would leave no trace behind. She explained to me her view of my husband's character—that he had become very stiff and unsociable. I agreed, and believed that I had learned to judge him myself more calmly and more truly.

But when I was alone with my husband later, the thought

that I had sat in judgement upon him weighed like a crime upon my conscience; and I felt that the gulf which divided us had grown still greater.

III

From that day there was a complete change in our life and our relations to each other. We were no longer as happy when we were alone together as before. To certain subjects we gave a wide berth, and conversation flowed more easily in the presence of a third person. When the talk turned on life in the country, or on a ball, we were uneasy and shrank from looking at one another. Both of us knew where the gulf between us lay, and seemed afraid to approach it. I was convinced that he was proud and irascible, and that I must be careful not to touch him on his weak point. He was equally sure that I disliked the country and was dying for social distraction, and that he must put up with this unfortunate taste of mine. We both avoided frank conversation on these topics, and each misjudged the other. We had long ceased to think each other the most perfect people in the world; each now judged the other in secret, and measured the offender by the standard of other people. I fell ill before we left Petersburg, and we went from there to a house near town, from which my husband went on alone, to join his mother at Nikól-skoe. By that time I was well enough to have gone with him, but he urged me to stay on the pretext of my health. I knew, however, that he was really afraid we should be uncomfortable together in the country; so I did not insist much, and he went off alone. I felt it dull and solitary in his absence; but when he came back, I saw that he did not add to my life what he had added formerly. In the old days every thought and experience weighed on me like a crime till I had imparted it to him; every action and word of his seemed to me a model of perfection; we often laughed for joy at the mere sight of each other. But these relations had changed, so imperceptibly that we had not even noticed their disappearance. Separate interests and cares, which we no longer tried to share, made their appearance, and even the fact of our estrangement ceased to trouble us. The idea became familiar, and, before a year had passed, each could look at the other without confusion. His fits of boyish merriment with me had quite vanished; his mood of calm indulgence to all that passed, which used to provoke me, had disappeared; there was an end of those penetrating looks which used to confuse and delight me, an end of the ecstasies and prayers which we once shared in common. We did not even meet often: he was continually absent, with no fears or regrets for leaving me alone; and I was constantly in society, where I did not need him.

There were no further scenes or quarrels between us. I tried to satisfy him, he carried out all my wishes, and we seemed to love each other.

When we were by ourselves, which we seldom were, I felt neither joy nor excitement nor embarrassment in his company: it seemed like being alone. I realized that he was my husband and no mere stranger, a good man, and as familiar to me as my own self. I was convinced that I knew just what he would say and do, and how he would look; and if anything he did surprised me, I concluded that he had made a mistake. I expected nothing from him. In a word, he was my husband—and that was all. It seemed to me that things must be so, as a matter of course, and that no other relations between us had ever existed. When he left home, especially at first, I was lonely and frightened and felt keenly my need of support; when he came back, I ran to his arms with joy, though two hours later my joy was quite forgotten, and I found nothing to say to him. Only at moments which sometimes occurred between us of quiet undemonstrative affection, I felt something wrong and some pain at my heart, and I seemed to read the same story in his eyes. I was conscious of a limit to tenderness, which he seemingly would not, and I could not, overstep. This saddened me sometimes; but I had no leisure to reflect on anything, and my regret for a change which I vaguely realized I tried to drown in the distractions which were always within my reach. Fashionable life, which had dazzled me at first by its glitter and flattery of my self-love, now took entire command of my nature, became a habit, laid its fetters upon me, and monopolized my capacity for feeling. I could not bear solitude, and was afraid to reflect on my position. My whole day, from late in the morning till late at night, was taken up by the claims of society; even if I stayed at home, my time was not my own. This no longer seemed to me either gay or dull, but it seemed that so, and not otherwise, it always had to be.

So three years passed, during which our relations to one another remained unchanged and seemed to have taken a fixed shape which could not become either better or worse. Though two events of importance in our family life took place during that time, neither of them changed my own life. These were the birth of my first child and the death of Tatyána Semënovna. At first the feeling of motherhood did take hold of me with such power, and produce in me such a passion of unanticipated joy, that I believed this would prove the beginning of a new life for me. But, in the course of two months, when I began to go out again, my feeling grew weaker and weaker, till it passed into mere habit and the lifeless performance of a duty. My husband, on the contrary, from the birth of our first boy, became his old self again—gentle, composed, and home-loving, and transferred to the child his old tenderness and gaiety. Many a night when I went, dressed for a ball, to the nursery, to sign the child with the cross before he slept, I found my husband there and felt his eyes fixed on me with something of reproof in their serious gaze. Then I was ashamed and even shocked by my own callousness, and asked myself if I was worse than other women. 'But it can't be helped,' I said to myself; 'I love my child, but to sit beside him all day long would bore me; and nothing will make me pretend what I do not really feel.'

His mother's death was a great sorrow to my husband; he said that he found it painful to go on living at Nikólskoe. For myself, although I mourned for her and sympathized with my husband's sorrow, yet I found life in that house easier and pleasanter after her death. Most of those three years we spent in town: I went only once to Nikólskoe for two months; and the third year we went abroad and spent the summer at Baden.

I was then twenty-one; our financial position was, I believed, satisfactory; my domestic life gave me all that I asked of it; everyone I knew, it seemed to me, loved me; my health was good; I was the best-dressed woman in Baden; I knew that I was good-looking; the weather was fine; I enjoyed the atmosphere of beauty and refinement; and, in short, I was in excellent spirits. They had once been even higher at Nikólskoe, when my happiness was in myself and came from the feeling that I deserved to be happy, and from the anticipation of still greater happiness to come. That was a different state of things; but I did very well this summer also. I had no special wishes or hopes or fears; it seemed to me that my life was full and my conscience easy. Among all the visitors at Baden that season there was no one man whom I preferred to the rest, or even to our old ambassador, Prince K., who was assiduous in his attentions to me. One was young, and another old; one was English and fair, another French and wore a beard—to me they were all alike, but all indispensable. Indistinguishable as they were, they together made up the atmosphere which I found so pleasant. But there was one, an Italian marquis, who stood out from the rest by reason of the boldness with which he expressed his admiration. He seized every opportunity of being with me—danced with me, rode with me, and met me at the casino; and everywhere he spoke to me of my charms. Several times I saw him from my windows loitering round our hotel, and the fixed gaze of his bright eyes often troubled me, and made me blush and turn away. He was young, handsome, and well-mannered; and, above all, by his smile and the expression of his brow, he resembled my husband, though much handsomer than he. He struck me by this likeness, though in general, in his lips, eyes, and long chin, there was something coarse and animal which contrasted with my husband's charming expression of kindness and noble serenity. I supposed him to be passionately in love with me, and thought of him sometimes with proud commiseration. When I tried at times to soothe him and change his tone to one of easy, half-friendly confidence, he resented the suggestion with vehemence, and continued to disquiet me by a smouldering passion which was ready at any moment to burst forth. Though I would not own it even to myself, I feared him and often thought of him against my will. My husband knew him, and treated him— even more than other acquaintances of ours who regarded him only as my husband—with coldness and disdain.

Towards the end of the season I fell ill and stayed indoors for a fortnight. The first evening that I went out again to hear the band, I learnt that Lady S., an Englishwoman famous for her beauty, who had long been expected, had arrived in my absence. My return was welcomed, and a group gathered round me; but a more distinguished group attended the beautiful stranger. She and her beauty were the one subject of conversation around me. When I saw her, she was really beautiful, but her self-satisfied expression struck me as disagreeable, and I said so. That day everything that had formerly seemed amusing, seemed dull. Lady S. arranged an expedition to the ruined castle for the next day; but I declined to be of the party. Almost everyone else went; and my opinion of Baden underwent a complete change. Everything and everybody seemed to me stupid and tiresome; I wanted to cry, to break off my cure, to return to Russia. There was some evil feeling in my soul, but I did not yet acknowledge it to myself. Pretending that I was not strong, I ceased to appear at crowded parties; if I went out, it was only in the morning by myself, to drink the waters; and my only companion was Mme M., a Russian lady, with whom I sometimes took drives in the surrounding country. My husband was absent: he had gone to Heidelberg for a time, intending to return to Russia when my cure was over, and only paid me occasional visits at Baden.

One day when Lady S. had carried off all the company on a hunting-expedition, Mme M. and I drove in the afternoon to the castle. While our carriage moved slowly along the winding road, bordered by ancient chestnut-trees and commanding a vista of the pretty and pleasant country round Baden, with the setting sun lighting it up, our conversation took a more serious turn than had ever happened to us before. I had known my companion for a long time; but she appeared to me now in a new light, as a well-principled and intelligent woman, to whom it was possible to speak without reserve, and whose friendship was worth having. We spoke of our private concerns, of our children, of the emptiness of life at Baden, till we felt a longing for Russia and the Russian countryside. When we entered the castle we were still under the impression of this serious feeling. Within the walls there was shade and coolness; the sunlight played from above upon the ruins. Steps and voices were audible. The landscape, charming enough but cold to a Russian eye, lay before us in the frame made by a doorway. We sat down to rest and watched the sunset in silence. The voices now sounded louder, and I thought I heard my own name. I listened and could not help overhearing every word. I recognized the voices: the speakers were the Italian marquis and a French friend of his whom I knew also. They were talking of me and of Lady S., and the Frenchman was comparing us as rival beauties. Though he said nothing insulting, his words made my pulse quicken. He explained in detail the good points of us both. I was already a mother, while Lady S. was only nineteen; though I had the advantage in hair, my rival had a better figure. 'Besides,' he added, 'Lady S. is a real *grande dame,* and the other is nothing in particular, only one of those obscure Russian princesses who turn up here nowadays in such numbers.' He ended by saying that I was wise in not attempting to compete with Lady S., and that I was completely buried as far as Baden was concerned.

'I am sorry for her—unless indeed she takes a fancy to console herself with you,' he added with a hard ringing laugh.

'If she goes away, I follow her'—the words were blurted out in an Italian accent.

'Happy man! he is still capable of a passion!' laughed the Frenchman.

'Passion!' said the other voice and then was still for a moment. 'It is a necessity to me: I cannot live without it. To make life a romance is the one thing worth doing. And with me romance never breaks off in the middle, and this affair I shall carry through to the end.'

Bonne chance, mon ami!' said the Frenchman.

They now turned a corner, and the voices stopped. Then we heard them coming down the steps, and a few minutes later they came out upon us by a side-door. They were much surprised to see us. I blushed when the marquis approached me, and felt afraid when we left the castle and he offered me his arm. I could not refuse, and we set off for the carriage, walking behind Mme M. and his friend. I was mortified by what the Frenchman had said of me, though I secretly admitted that he had only put in words what I felt myself; but the plain speaking of the Italian had surprised and upset me by its coarseness. I was tormented by the thought that, though I had overheard him, he showed no fear of me. It was hateful to have him so close to me; and I walked fast after the other couple, not looking at him or answering him and trying to hold his arm in such a way as not to hear him. He spoke of the fine view, of the unexpected pleasure of our meeting, and so on; but I was not listening. My thoughts were with my husband, my child, my country; I felt ashamed, distressed, anxious; I was in a hurry to get back to my solitary room in the Hôtel de Bade, there to think at leisure of the storm of feeling that had just risen in my heart. But Mme M. walked slowly, it was still a long way to the carriage, and my escort seemed to loiter on purpose as if he wished to detain me. 'None of that!' I thought, and resolutely quickened my pace. But it soon became unmistakable that he was detaining me and even pressing my arm. Mme M. turned a corner, and we were quite alone. I was afraid.

'Excuse me,' I said coldly and tried to free my arm; but the lace of my sleeve caught on a button of his coat. Bending towards me, he began to unfasten it, and his ungloved fingers touched my arm. A feeling new to me, half horror and half pleasure, sent an icy shiver down my back. I looked at him, intending by my coldness to convey all the contempt I felt for him; but my look expressed nothing but fear and excitement. His liquid blazing eyes, right up against my face, stared strangely at me, at my neck and breast; both his hands fingered my arm above the wrist; his parted lips were saying that he loved me, and that I was all the world to him; and those lips were coming nearer and nearer, and those hands were squeezing mine harder and harder and burning me. A fever ran through my veins, my sight grew dim, I trembled, and the words intended to check him died in my throat. Suddenly I felt a kiss on my cheek. Trembling all over and turning cold, I stood still and stared at him. Unable to speak or move, I stood there, horrified, expectant, even desirous. It was over in a moment, but the moment was horrible! In that short time I saw him exactly as he was—the low straight forehead (that forehead so like my husband's!) under the straw hat; the handsome regular nose and dilated nostrils; the long waxed moustache and short beard; the close-shaved cheeks and sunburnt neck. I hated and feared him; he was utterly repugnant and alien to me. And yet the excitement and passion of this hateful strange man raised a powerful echo in my own heart; I felt an irresistible longing to surrender myself to the kisses of that coarse handsome mouth, and to the pressure of those white hands with their delicate veins and jewelled fingers; I was tempted to throw myself headlong into the abyss of forbidden delights that had suddenly opened up before me.

'I am so unhappy already,' I thought; 'let more and more storms of unhappiness burst over my head!'

He put one arm round me and bent towards my face. 'Better so!' I thought: 'let sin and shame cover me ever deeper and deeper!'

'Je vous aimer!' he whispered in the voice which was so like my husband's. At once I thought of my husband and child, as creatures once precious to me who had now passed altogether out of my life. At that moment I heard Mme M.'s voice; she called to me from round the corner. I came to myself, tore my hand away without looking at him, and almost ran after her: I only looked at him after she and I were already seated in the carriage. Then I saw him raise his hat and ask some commonplace question with a smile. He little knew the inexpressible aversion I felt for him at that moment.

My life seemed so wretched, the future so hopeless, the past so black! When Mme M. spoke, her words meant nothing to me. I thought that she talked only out of pity, and to hide the contempt I aroused in her. In every word and every look I seemed to detect this contempt and insulting pity. The shame of that kiss burnt my cheek, and the thought of my husband and child was more than I could bear. When I was alone in my own room, I tried to think over my position; but I was afraid to be alone. Without drinking the tea which was brought me, and uncertain of my own motives, I got ready with feverish haste to catch the evening train and join my husband at Heidelberg.

I found seats for myself and my maid in an empty carriage. When the train started and the fresh air blew through the window on my face, I grew more composed and pictured my past and future to myself more clearly. The course of our married life from the time of our first visit to Petersburg now presented itself to me in a new light, and lay like a reproach on my conscience. For the first time I clearly recalled our start at Nikólskoe and our plans for the future; and for the first time I asked myself what happiness had my husband had since then. I felt that I had behaved badly to him. 'But why', I asked myself, 'did he not stop me? Why did he make pretences? Why did he always avoid explanations? Why did he insult me? Why did he not use the power of his love to influence me? Or did he not love me?' But whether he was to blame or not, I still felt the kiss of that strange man upon my cheek. The nearer we got to Heidelberg, the clearer grew my picture of my husband, and the more I dreaded our meeting. 'I shall tell him all,' I thought, 'and wipe out everything with tears of repentance; and he will forgive me.' But I did not know myself what I meant by 'everything'; and I did not believe in my heart that he would forgive me.

As soon as I entered my husband's room and saw his calm though surprised expression, I felt at once that I had nothing to tell him, no confession to make, and nothing to ask forgiveness for. I had to suppress my unspoken grief and penitence.

'What put this into your head?' he asked. 'I meant to go to Baden to-morrow.' Then he looked more closely at me and seemed to take alarm. 'What's the matter with you? What has happened?' he said.

'Nothing at all,' I replied, almost breaking down. 'I am not going back. Let us go home, to-morrow if you like, to Russia.'

For some time he said nothing but looked at me attentively. Then he said, 'But do tell me what has happened to you.'

I blushed involuntarily and looked down. There came into his eyes a flash of anger and displeasure. Afraid of what he might imagine, I said with a power of pretence that surprised myself:

'Nothing at all has happened. It was merely that I grew weary and sad by myself; and I have been thinking a great deal of our way of life and of you. I have long been to blame towards you. Why do you take me abroad, when you can't bear it yourself? I have long been to blame. Let us go back to Nikólskoe and settle there for ever.'

'Spare us these sentimental scenes, my dear,' he said coldly. 'To go back to Nikólskoe is a good idea, for our money is running short; but the notion of stopping there "for ever" is fanciful. I know you would not settle down. Have some tea, and you will feel better,' and he rose to ring for the waiter.

I imagined all he might be thinking about me; and I was offended by the horrible thoughts which I ascribed to him when I encountered the dubious and shame-faced look he directed at me. 'He will not and cannot understand me.' I said I would go and look at the child, and I left the room. I wished to be alone, and to cry and cry and cry. . .

IV

The house at Nikólskoe, so long unheated and uninhabited, came to life again; but much of the past was dead beyond recall. Tatyána Semënovna was no more, and we were now alone together. But far from desiring such close companionship, we even found it irksome. To me that winter was the more trying because I was in bad health, from which I only recovered after the birth of my second son. My husband and I were still on the same terms as during our life in Petersburg: we were coldly friendly to each other, but in the country each room and wall and sofa recalled what he had once been to me, and what I had lost. It was as if some unforgiven grievance held us apart, as if he were punishing me and pretending not to be aware of it. But there was nothing to ask pardon for, no penalty to deprecate; my punishment was merely this, that he did not give his whole heart and mind to me as he used to do; but he did not give it to anyone or to anything; as though he had no longer a heart to give. Sometimes it occurred to me that he was only pretending to be like that, in order to hurt me, and that the old feeling was still alive in his breast; and I tried to call it forth. But I always failed: he always seemed to avoid frankness, evidently suspecting me of insincerity, and dreading the folly of any emotional display. I could read in his face and the tone of his voice, 'What is the good of talking? I know all the facts already, and I know what is on the tip of your tongue, and I know that you will say one thing and do another.' At first I was mortified by his dread of frankness, but I came later to think that it was rather the absence, on his part, of any need of frankness. It would never have occurred to me now, to tell him of a sudden that I loved him, or to ask him to repeat the prayers with me or listen while I played the piano. Our intercourse came to be regulated by a fixed code of good manners. We lived our separate lives: he had his own occupations in which I was not needed, and which I no longer wished to share, while I continued my idle life which no longer vexed or grieved him. The children were still too young to form a bond between us.

But spring came round and brought Kátya and Sónya to spend the summer with us in the country. As the house at Nikólskoe was under repair, we went to live at my old home at Pokróvskoe. The old house was unchanged— the veranda, the folding table and the piano in the sunny drawing-room, and my old bedroom with its white curtains and the dreams of my girlhood which I seemed to have left behind me there. In that room there were two beds: one had been mine, and in it now my plump little Kokósha lay sprawling, when I went at night to sign him with the cross; the other was a crib, in which the little face of my baby, Ványa, peeped out from his swaddling-clothes. Often, when I had made the sign over them and remained standing in the middle of the quiet room, suddenly there rose up from all the corners, from the walls and curtains, old forgotten visions of youth. Old voices began to sing the songs of my girlhood. Where were those visions now? where were those dear old sweet songs? All that I had hardly dared to hope for had come to pass. My vague confused dreams had become a reality, and the reality had become an oppressive, difficult, and joyless life. All remained the same—the garden visible through the window, the grass, the path, the very same bench over there above the dell, the same song of the nightingale by the pond, the same lilacs in full bloom, the same moon shining above the house; and yet, in everything such a terrible inconceivable change! Such coldness in all that might have been near and dear! Just as in old times, Kátya and I sit quietly alone together in the parlour and talk, and talk of him. But Kátya has grown wrinkled and pale; and her eyes no longer shine with joy and hope, but express only sympathy, sorrow, and regret. We do not go into raptures as we used to, we judge him coolly; we do not wonder what we have done to deserve such happiness, or long to proclaim our thoughts to all the world. No! we whisper together like conspirators and ask each other for the hundredth time why all has changed so sadly. Yet he was still the same man, save for the deeper furrow between his eyebrows and the whiter hair on his temples; but his serious attentive look was constantly veiled from me by a cloud. And I am the same woman, but without love or desire for love, with no longing for work and no content with myself. My religious ecstasies, my love for my husband, the fullness of my former life—all these now seem utterly remote and visionary. Once it seemed so plain and right that to live for others was happiness; but now it has become unintelligible. Why live for others, when life had no attraction even for oneself?

I had given up my music altogether since the time of our first visit to Petersburg; but now the old piano and the old music tempted me to begin again.

One day I was not well and stayed indoors alone. My husband had taken Kátya and Sónya to see the new buildings at Nikólskoe. Tea was laid; I went downstairs and while waiting for them sat down at the piano. I opened the 'Moonlight Sonata' and began to play. There was no one within sight or sound, the windows were open over the garden, and the familiar sounds floated through the room with a solemn sadness. At the end of the first movement I looked round instinctively to the corner where he used once to sit and listen to my playing. He was not there; his chair, long unmoved, was still in its place; through the window I could see a lilac-bush against the light of the setting sun; the freshness of evening streamed in through the open windows. I rested my elbows on the piano and covered my face with both hands; and so I sat for a long time, thinking. I recalled with pain the irrevocable past, and timidly imagined the future. But for me there seemed to be no future, no desires at all and no hopes. 'Can life be over for me?' I thought with horror; then I looked up, and, trying to forget and not to think, I began playing the same movement over again. 'O God!' I prayed, 'forgive me if I have sinned, or restore to me all that once blossomed in my heart, or teach me what to do and how to live now.' There was a sound of wheels on the grass and before the steps of the house; then I heard cautious and familiar foot-steps pass along the veranda and cease; but my heart no longer replied to the sound. When I stopped playing the footsteps were behind me and a hand was laid on my shoulder.

'How clever of you to think of playing that!' he said.

I said nothing.

'Have you had tea?' he asked.

I shook my head without looking at him—I was unwilling to let him see the signs of emotion on my face.

'They'll be here immediately,' he said; 'the horse gave trouble, and they got out on the high road to walk home.'

'Let us wait for them,' I said, and went out to the veranda, hoping that he would follow; but he asked about the children and went upstairs to see them. Once more his presence and simple kindly voice made me doubt if I had really lost anything. What more could I wish? 'He is kind and gentle, a good husband, a good father; I don't know myself what more I want.' I sat down under the veranda awning on the very bench on which I had sat when we became engaged. The sun had set, it was growing dark, and a little spring rain-cloud hung over the house and garden, and only behind the trees the horizon was clear, with the fading glow of twilight, in which one star had just begun to twinkle. The landscape, covered by the shadow of the cloud, seemed waiting for the light spring shower. There was not a breath of wind; not a single leaf or blade of grass stirred; the scent of lilac and bird-cherry was so strong in the garden and veranda that it seemed as if all the air was in flower; it came in wafts, now stronger and now weaker, till one longed to shut both eyes and ears and drink in that fragrance only. The dahlias and rose-bushes, not yet in flower, stood motionless on the black mould of the border, looking as if they were growing slowly upwards on their white-shaved props; beyond the dell, the frogs were making the most of their time before the rain drove them to the pond, croaking busily and loudly. Only the high continuous note of water falling at some distance rose above their croaking. From time to time the nightingales called to one another, and I could hear them flitting restlessly from bush to bush. Again this spring a nightingale had tried to build in a bush under the window, and I heard her fly off across the avenue when I went into the veranda. From there she whistled once and then stopped; she, too, was expecting the rain.

I tried in vain to calm my feelings: I had a sense of anticipation and regret.

He came downstairs again and sat down beside me.

'I am afraid they will get wet,' he said.

'Yes,' I answered; and we sat for long without speaking.

The cloud came down lower and lower with no wind. The air grew stiller and more fragrant Suddenly a drop fell on the canvas awning and seemed to rebound from it; then another broke on the gravel path; soon there was a splash on the burdock leaves, and a fresh shower of big drops came down faster and faster. Nightingales and frogs were both dumb; only the high note of the falling water, though the rain made it seem more distant, still went on; and a bird, which must have sheltered among the dry leaves near the veranda, steadily repeated its two unvarying notes. My husband got up to go in.

'Where are you going?' I asked, trying to keep him; 'it is so pleasant here.'

'We must send them an umbrella and goloshes,' he replied.

'Don't trouble—it will soon be over.'

He thought I was right, and we remained together in the veranda. I rested one hand upon the wet slippery rail and put my head out. The fresh rain wetted my hair and neck in places. The cloud, growing lighter and thinner, was passing overhead; the steady patter of the rain gave place to occasional drops that fell from the sky or dripped from the trees. The frogs began to croak again in the dell; the nightingales woke up and began to call from the dripping bushes from one side and then from another. The whole prospect before us grew clear.

'How delightful!' he said, seating himself on the veranda rail and passing a hand over my wet hair.

This simple caress had on me the effect of a reproach: I felt inclined to cry.

'What more can a man need?' he said; 'I am so content now that I want nothing; I am perfectly happy!'

He told me a different story once, I thought. He had said that, however great his happiness might be, he always wanted more and more. Now he is calm and contented; while my heart is full of unspoken repentance and unshed tears.

'I think it delightful too,' I said; 'but I am sad just because of the beauty of it all. All is so fair and lovely outside me, while my own heart is confused and baffled and full of vague unsatisfied longing. Is it possible that there is no element of pain, no yearning for the past, in your enjoyment of nature?'

He took his hand off my head and was silent for a little.

'I used to feel that too,' he said, as though recalling it, 'especially in spring. I used to sit up all night too, with my hopes and fears for company, and good company they were! But life was all before me then. Now it is all behind me, and I am content with what I have. I find life capital,' he added with such careless confidence, that I believed, whatever pain it gave me to hear it, that it was the truth.

'But is there nothing you wish for?' I asked.

'I don't ask for impossibilities,' he said, guessing my thoughts. 'You go and get your head wet,' he added, stroking my head like a child's and again passing his hand over the wet hair; 'you envy the leaves and the grass their wetting from the rain, and you would like yourself to be the grass and the leaves and the rain. But I am content to enjoy them and everything else that is good and young and happy.'

'And do you regret nothing of the past?' I asked, while my heart grew heavier and heavier.

Again he thought for a time before replying. I saw that he wished to reply with perfect frankness.

'Nothing,' he said shortly.

'Not true! not true!' I said, turning towards him and looking into his eyes. 'Do you really not regret the past?'

'No!' he repeated; 'I am grateful for it, but I don't regret it.'

'But would you not like to have it back?' I asked.

He turned away and looked out over the garden.

'No; I might as well wish to have wings. It is impossible.'

'And would you not alter the past? do you not reproach yourself or me?'

'No, never! It was all for the best.'

'Listen to me!' I said touching his arm to make him look round. 'Why did you never tell me that you wished me to live as you really wished me to? Why did you give me a freedom for which I was unfit? Why did you stop teaching me? If you had wished it, if you had guided me differently, none of all this would have happened!' said I in a voice that increasingly expressed cold displeasure and reproach in place of the love of former days.

'What would not have happened?' he asked, turning to me in surprise. 'As it is, there is nothing wrong. Things are all right, quite all right,' he added with a smile.

'Does he really not understand?' I thought; 'or still worse, does he not wish to understand?'

Then I suddenly broke out. 'Had you acted differently, I should not now be punished, for no fault at all, by your indifference and even contempt, and you would not have taken from me unjustly all that I valued in life!'

'What do you mean, my dear one?' he asked—he seemed not to understand me.

'No! don't interrupt me! You have taken from me your confidence, your love, even your respect; for I cannot believe, when I think of the past, that you still love me. No! don't speak! I must once for all say out what has long been torturing me. Is it my fault that I knew nothing of life, and that you left me to learn experience for myself? Is it my fault that now, when I have gained the knowledge and have been struggling for nearly a year to come back to you, you push me away and pretend not to understand what I want? And you always do it so that it is impossible to reproach you, while I am guilty and unhappy. Yes, you wish to drive me out again to that life which might rob us both of happiness.'

'How did I show that?' he asked in evident alarm and surprise.

'No later than yesterday you said, and you constantly say, that I can never settle down here, and that we must spend this winter too at Petersburg; and I hate Petersburg!' I went on. 'Instead of supporting me, you avoid all plain speaking, you never say a single frank affectionate word to me. And then, when I fall utterly, you will reproach me and rejoice in my fall.'

'Stop!' he said with cold severity. 'You have no right to say that. It only proves that you are ill-disposed towards me, that you don't . . .'

'That I don't love you? Don't hesitate to say it!' I cried, and the tears began to flow. I sat down on the bench and covered my face with my handkerchief.

'So that is how he understood me!' I thought, trying to restrain the sobs which choked me. 'Gone, gone is our former love!' said a voice at my heart. He did not come close or try to comfort me. He was hurt by what I had said. When he spoke, his tone was cool and dry.

'I don't know what you reproach me with,' he began. 'If you mean that I don't love you as I once did . . .'

'Did love!' I said, with my face buried in the handkerchief, while the bitter tears fell still more abundantly.

'If so, time is to blame for that, and we ourselves. Each time of life has its own kind of love.' He was silent for a moment. 'Shall I tell you the whole truth, if you really wish for frankness? In that summer when I first knew you, I used to lie awake all night, thinking about you, and I made that love myself, and it grew and grew in my heart. So again, in Petersburg and abroad, in the course of horrible sleepless nights, I strove to shatter and destroy that love, which had come to torture me. I did not destroy it, but I destroyed that part of it which gave me pain. Then I grew calm; and I feel love still, but it is a different kind of love.'

'You call it love, but I call it torture!' I said. 'Why did you allow me to go into society, if you thought so badly of it that you ceased to love me on that account?'

'No, it was not society, my dear,' he said.

'Why did you not exercise your authority?' I went on: 'why did you not lock me up or kill me? That would have been better than the loss of all that formed my happiness. I should have been happy, instead of being ashamed.'

I began to sob again and hid my face.

Just then Kátya and Sónya, wet and cheerful, came out to the veranda, laughing and talking loudly. They were silent as soon as they saw us, and went in again immediately.

We remained silent for a long time. I had had my cry out and felt relieved. I glanced at him. He was sitting with his head resting on his hand; he intended to make some reply to my glance, but only sighed deeply and resumed his former position.

I went up to him and removed his hand. His eyes turned thoughtfully to my face.

'Yes,' he began, as if continuing his thoughts aloud, 'all of us, and especially you women, must have personal experience of all the nonsense of life, in order to get back to life itself; the evidence of other people is no good. At that time you had not got near the end of that charming nonsense which I admired in you. So I let you go through it alone, feeling that I had no right to put pressure on you, though my own time for that sort of thing was long past.'

'If you loved me,' I said, 'how could you stand beside me and suffer me to go through it?'

'Because it was impossible for you to take my word for it, though you would have tried to. Personal experience was necessary, and now you have had it.'

'There was much calculation in all that,' I said, 'but little love.'

Again we were silent.

'What you said just now is severe, but it is true,' he began, rising suddenly and beginning to walk about the veranda. 'Yes, it is true. I was to blame,' he added, stopping opposite me; 'I ought either to have kept myself from loving you at all, or to have loved you in a simpler way.'

'Let us forget it all,' I said timidly.

'No,' he said; 'the past can never come back, never;' and his voice softened as he spoke.

'It is restored already,' I said, laying a hand on his shoulder.

He took my hand away and pressed it.

'I was wrong when I said that I did not regret the past. I do regret it; I weep for that past love which can never return. Who is to blame, I do not know. Love remains, but not the old love; its place remains, but it is all wasted away and has lost all strength and substance; recollections are still left, and gratitude; but . . .'

'Do not say that!' I broke in. 'Let all be as it was before! Surely that is possible?' I asked, looking into his eyes; but their gaze was clear and calm, and did not look deeply into mine.

Even while I spoke, I knew that my wishes and my petition were impossible. He smiled calmly and gently; and I thought it the smile of an old man.

'How young you are still!' he said, 'and I am so old. What you seek in me is no longer there. Why deceive ourselves?' he added, still smiling.

I stood silent opposite to him, and my heart grew calmer.

'Don't let us try to repeat life,' he went on. 'Don't let us make pretences to ourselves. Let us be thankful that there is an end of the old emotions and excitements. The excitement of searching is over for us; our quest is done, and happiness enough has fallen to our lot. Now we must stand aside and make room— for him, if you like,' he said, pointing to the nurse who was carrying Ványa out and had stopped at the veranda door. 'That's the truth, my dear one,' he said, drawing down my head and kissing it, not a lover any longer but an old friend.

The fragrant freshness of the night rose ever stronger and sweeter from the garden; the sounds and the silence grew more solemn; star after star began to twinkle overhead. I looked at him, and suddenly my heart grew light; it seemed that the cause of my suffering had been removed like an aching nerve. Suddenly I realized clearly and calmly that the past feeling, like the past time itself, was gone beyond recall, and that it would be not only impossible but painful and uncomfortable to bring it back. And after all, was that time so good which seemed to me so happy? And it was all so long, long ago!

'Time for tea!' he said, and we went together to the parlour. At the door we met the nurse with the baby. I took him in my arms, covered his bare little red legs, pressed him to me, and kissed him with the lightest touch of my lips. Half asleep, he moved the parted fingers of one creased little hand and opened dim little eyes, as if he was looking for something or recalling something. All at once his eyes rested on me, a spark of consciousness shone in them, the little pouting lips, parted before, now met and opened in a smile. 'Mine, mine, mine!' I thought, pressing him to my breast with such an impulse of joy in every limb that I found it hard to restrain myself from hurting him. I fell to kissing the cold little feet, his stomach and hand and head with its thin covering of down. My husband came up to me, and I quickly covered the child's face and uncovered it again.

'Iván Sergéich!' said my husband, tickling him under the chin. But I made haste to cover Iván Sergéich up again. None but I had any business to look long at him. I glanced at my husband. His eyes smiled as he looked at me; and I looked into them with an ease and happiness which I had not felt for a long time.

That day ended the romance of our marriage; the old feeling became a precious irrecoverable remembrance; but a new feeling of love for my children and the father of my children laid the foundation of a new life and a quite different happiness; and that life and happiness have lasted to the present time.

MASTER AND MAN

[1895]

I

It happened in the 'seventies in winter, on the day after St. Nicholas's Day. There was a fête in the parish and the innkeeper, Vasíli Andréevich Brekhunóv, a Second Guild merchant, being a church elder had to go to church, and had also to entertain his relatives and friends at home.

But when the last of them had gone he at once began to prepare to drive over to see a neighbouring proprietor about a grove which he had been bargaining over for a long time. He was now in a hurry to start, lest buyers from the town might forestall him in making a profitable purchase.

The youthful landowner was asking ten thousand rubles for the grove simply because Vasíli Andréevich was offering seven thousand. Seven thousand was, however, only a third of its real value. Vasíli Andréevich might perhaps have got it down to his own price, for the woods were in his district and he had a long-standing agreement with the other village dealers that no one should run up the price in another's district, but he had now learnt that some timber-dealers from town meant to bid for the Goryáchkin grove, and he resolved to go at once and get the matter settled. So as soon as the feast was over, he took seven hundred rubles from his strong box, added to them two thousand three hundred rubles of church money he had in his keeping, so as to make up the sum to three thousand; carefully counted the notes, and having put them into his pocket-book made haste to start.

Nikíta, the only one of Vasíli Andréevich's labourers who was not drunk that day, ran to harness the horse. Nikíta, though an habitual drunkard, was not drunk that day because since the last day before the fast, when he had drunk his coat and leather boots, he had sworn off drink and had kept his vow for two months, and was still keeping it despite the temptation of the vodka that had been drunk everywhere during the first two days of the feast.

Nikíta was a peasant of about fifty from a neighbouring village, 'not a manager' as the peasants said of him, meaning that he was not the thrifty head of a household but lived most of his time away from home as a labourer. He was valued everywhere for his industry, dexterity, and strength at work, and still more for his kindly and pleasant temper. But he never settled down anywhere for long because about twice a year, or even oftener, he had a drinking bout, and then besides spending all his clothes on drink he became turbulent and quarrelsome. Vasíli Andréevich himself had turned him away several times, but had afterwards taken him back again—valuing his honesty, his kindness to animals, and especially his cheapness. Vasíli Andréevich did not pay Nikíta the eighty rubles a year such a man was worth, but only about forty, which he gave him haphazard, in small sums, and even that mostly not in cash but in goods from his own shop and at high prices.

Nikíta's wife Martha, who had once been a handsome vigorous woman, managed the homestead with the help of her son and two daughters, and did not urge Nikíta to live at home: first because she had been living for some twenty years already with a cooper, a peasant from another village who lodged in their house; and secondly because though she managed her husband as she pleased when he was sober, she feared him like fire when he was drunk. Once when he had got drunk at home, Nikíta, probably to make up for his submissiveness when sober, broke open her box, took out her best clothes, snatched up an axe, and chopped all her undergarments and dresses to bits. All the wages Nikíta earned went to his wife, and he raised no objection to that. So now, two days before the holiday, Martha had been twice to see Vasíli Andréevich and had got from him wheat flour, tea, sugar, and a quart of vodka, the lot costing three rubles, and also five rubles in cash, for which she thanked him as for a special favour, though he owed Nikíta at least twenty rubles.

'What agreement did we ever draw up with you?' said Vasíli Andréevich to Nikíta. 'If you need anything, take it; you will work it off. I'm not like others to keep you waiting, and making up accounts and reckoning fines. We deal straight-forwardly. You serve me and I don't neglect you.'

And when saying this Vasíli Andréevich was honestly convinced that he was Nikíta's benefactor, and he knew how to put it so plausibly that all those who depended on him for their money, beginning with Nikíta, confirmed him in the conviction that he was their benefactor and did not overreach them.

'Yes, I understand, Vasíli Andréevich. You know that I serve you and take as much pains as I would for my own father. I understand very well!' Nikíta would reply. He was quite aware that Vasíli Andréevich was cheating him, but at the same time he felt that it was useless to try to clear up his accounts with him or explain his side of the matter, and that as long as he had nowhere to go he must accept what he could get.

Now, having heard his master's order to harness, he went as usual cheerfully and willingly to the shed, stepping briskly and easily on his rather turned-in feet; took down from a nail the heavy tasselled leather bridle, and jingling the rings of the bit went to the closed stable where the horse he was to harness was standing by himself.

'What, feeling lonely, feeling lonely, little silly?' said Nikíta in answer to the low whinny with which he was greeted by the good-tempered, medium-sized bay stallion, with a rather slanting crupper, who stood alone in the shed. 'Now then, now then, there's time enough. Let me water you first,' he went on, speaking to the horse just as to someone who understood the words he was using, and having whisked the dusty, grooved back of the well-fed young stallion with the skirt of his coat, he put a bridle on his handsome head, straightened his ears and forelock, and having taken off his halter led him out to water.

Picking his way out of the dung-strewn stable, Mukhórty frisked, and making play with his hind leg pretended that he meant to kick Nikíta, who was running at a trot beside him to the pump.

'Now then, now then, you rascal!' Nikíta called out, well knowing how carefully Mukhórty threw out his hind leg just to touch his greasy sheepskin coat but not to strike him—a trick Nikíta much appreciated.

After a drink of the cold water the horse sighed, moving his strong wet lips, from the hairs of which transparent drops fell into the trough; then standing still as if in thought, he suddenly gave a loud snort.

'If you don't want any more, you needn't. But don't go asking for any later,' said Nikíta quite seriously and fully explaining his conduct to Mukhórty. Then he ran back to the shed pulling the playful young horse, who wanted to gambol all over the yard, by the rein.

There was no one else in the yard except a stranger, the cook's husband, who had come for the holiday.

'Go and ask which sledge is to be harnessed—the wide one or the small one—there's a good fellow!'

The cook's husband went into the house, which stood on an iron foundation and was iron-roofed, and soon returned saying that the little one was to be harnessed. By that time Nikíta had put the collar and brass-studded belly-band on Mukhórty and, carrying a light, painted shaft-bow in one hand, was leading the horse with the other up to two sledges that stood in the shed.

'All right, let it be the little one!' he said, backing the intelligent horse, which all the time kept pretending to bite him, into the shafts, and with the aid of the cook's husband he proceeded to harness. When everything was nearly ready and only the reins had to be adjusted, Nikíta sent the other man to the shed for some straw and to the barn for a drugget.

'There, that's all right! Now, now, don't bristle up!' said Nikíta, pressing down into the sledge the freshly threshed oat straw the cook's husband had brought 'And now let's spread the sacking like this, and the drugget over it. There, like that it will be comfortable sitting,' he went on, suiting the action to the words and tucking the drugget all round over the straw to make a seat.

'Thank you, dear man. Things always go quicker with two working at it!' he added. And gathering up the leather reins fastened together by a brass ring, Nikíta took the driver's seat and started the impatient horse over the frozen manure which lay in the yard, towards the gate.

'Uncle Nikíta! I say, Uncle, Uncle!' a high-pitched voice shouted, and a seven-year-old boy in a black sheepskin coat, new white felt boots, and a warm cap, ran hurriedly out of the house into the yard. 'Take me with you!' he cried, fastening up his coat as he ran.

'All right, come along, darling!' said Nikíta, and stopping the sledge he picked up the master's pale thin little son, radiant with joy, and drove out into the road.

It was past two o'clock and the day was windy, dull, and cold, with more than twenty degrees Fahrenheit of frost. Half the sky was hidden by a lowering dark cloud. In the yard it was quiet, but in the street the wind was felt more keenly. The snow swept down from a neighbouring shed and whirled about in the corner near the bath-house.

Hardly had Nikíta driven out of the yard and turned the horse's head to the house, before Vasíli Andréevich emerged from the high porch in front of the house with a cigarette in his mouth and wearing a cloth-covered sheepskin coat tightly girdled low at his waist, and stepped onto the hard-trodden snow which squeaked under the leather soles of his felt boots, and stopped. Taking a last whiff of his cigarette he threw it down, stepped on it, and letting the smoke escape through his moustache and looking askance at the horse that was coming up, began to tuck in his sheepskin collar on both sides of his ruddy face, clean-shaven except for the moustache, so that his breath should not moisten the collar.

'See now! The young scamp is there already!' he exclaimed when he saw his little son in the sledge. Vasíli Andréevich was excited by the vodka he had drunk with his visitors, and so he was even more pleased than usual with everything that was his and all that he did. The sight of his son, whom he always thought of as his heir, now gave him great satisfaction. He looked at him, screwing up his eyes and showing his long teeth.

His wife—pregnant, thin and pale, with her head and shoulders wrapped in a shawl so that nothing of her face could be seen but her eyes—stood behind him in the vestibule to see him off.

'Now really, you ought to take Nikíta with you,' she said timidly, stepping out from the doorway.

Vasíli Andréevich did not answer. Her words evidently annoyed him and he frowned angrily and spat.

'You have money on you,' she continued in the same plaintive voice. 'What if the weather gets worse! Do take him, for goodness' sake!'

'Why? Don't I know the road that I must needs take a guide?' exclaimed Vasíli Andréevich, uttering every word very distinctly and compressing his lips unnaturally, as he usually did when speaking to buyers and sellers.

'Really you ought to take him. I beg you in God's name!' his wife repeated, wrapping her shawl more closely round her head.

'There, she sticks to it like a leech! . . . Where am I to take him?'

'I'm quite ready to go with you, Vasíli Andréevich,' said Nikíta cheerfully. 'But they must feed the horses while I am away,' he added, turning to his master's wife.

'I'll look after them, Nikíta dear. I'll tell Simon,' replied the mistress.

'Well, Vasíli Andréevich, am I to come with you?' said Nikíta, awaiting a decision.

'It seems I must humour my old woman. But if you're coming you'd better put on a warmer cloak,' said Vasíli Andréevich, smiling again as he winked at Nikíta's short sheepskin coat, which was torn under the arms and at the back, was greasy and out of shape, frayed to a fringe round the skirt, and had endured many things in its lifetime.

'Hey, dear man, come and hold the horse!' shouted Nikíta to the cook's husband, who was still in the yard.

'No, I will myself, I will myself!' shrieked the little boy, pulling his hands, red with cold, out of his pockets, and seizing the cold leather reins.

'Only don't be too long dressing yourself up. Look alive!' shouted Vasíli Andréevich, grinning at Nikíta.

'Only a moment, Father, Vasíli Andréevich!' replied Nikíta, and running quickly with his inturned toes in his felt boots with their soles patched with felt, he hurried across the yard and into the workmen's hut.

'Arínushka! Get my coat down from the stove. I'm going with the master,' he said, as he ran into the hut and took down his girdle from the nail on which it hung.

The workmen's cook, who had had a sleep after dinner and was now getting the samovar ready for her husband, turned cheerfully to Nikíta, and infected by his hurry began to move as quickly as he did, got down his miserable worn-out cloth coat from the stove where it was drying, and began hurriedly shaking it out and smoothing it down.

'There now, you'll have a chance of a holiday with your good man,' said Nikíta, who from kindhearted politeness always said something to anyone he was alone with.

Then, drawing his worn narrow girdle round him, he drew in his breath, pulling in his lean stomach still more, and girdled himself as tightly as he could over his sheepskin.

'There now,' he said addressing himself no longer to the cook but the girdle, as he tucked the ends in at the waist, 'now you won't come undone!' And working his shoulders up and down to free his arms, he put the coat over his sheepskin, arched his back more strongly to ease his arms, poked himself under the armpits, and took down his leather-covered mittens from the shelf. 'Now we're all right!'

'You ought to wrap your feet up, Nikíta. Your boots are very bad.'

Nikíta stopped as if he had suddenly realized this.

'Yes, I ought to. . . . But they'll do like this. It isn't far!' and he ran out into the yard.

'Won't you be cold, Nikíta?' said the mistress as he came up to the sledge.

'Cold? No, I'm quite warm,' answered Nikíta as he pushed some straw up to the forepart of the sledge so that it should cover his feet, and stowed away the whip, which the good horse would not need, at the bottom of the sledge.

Vasíli Andréevich, who was wearing two fur-lined coats one over the other, was already in the sledge, his broad back filling nearly its whole rounded width, and taking the reins he immediately touched the horse. Nikíta jumped in just as the sledge started, and seated himself in front on the left side, with one leg hanging over the edge.

II

The good stallion took the sledge along at a brisk pace over the smooth-frozen road through the village, the runners squeaking slightly as they went.

'Look at him hanging on there! Hand me the whip, Nikíta!' shouted Vasíli Andréevich, evidently enjoying the sight of his 'heir,' who standing on the runners was hanging on at the back of the sledge. 'I'll give it you! Be off to mamma, you dog!'

The boy jumped down. The horse increased his amble and, suddenly changing foot, broke into a fast trot.

The Crosses, the village where Vasíli Andréevich lived, consisted of six houses. As soon as they had passed the blacksmith's hut, the last in the village, they realized that the wind was much stronger than they had thought. The road could hardly be seen. The tracks left by the sledge-runners were immediately covered by snow and the road was only distinguished by the fact that it was higher than the rest of the ground. There was a whirl of snow over the fields and the line where sky and earth met could not be seen. The Telyátin forest, usually clearly visible, now only loomed up occasionally and dimly through the driving snowy dust. The wind came from the left, insistently blowing over to one side the mane on Mukhórty's sleek neck and carrying aside even his fluffy tail, which was tied in a simple knot. Nikíta's wide coat-collar, as he sat on the windy side, pressed close to his cheek and nose.

'This road doesn't give him a chance—it's too snowy,' said Vasíli Andréevich, who prided himself on his good horse. 'I once drove to Pashútino with him in half an hour.'

'What? asked Nikíta, who could not hear on account of his collar.

'I say I once went to Pashútino in half an hour,' shouted Vasíli Andréevich.

'It goes without saying that he's a good horse,' replied Nikíta.

They were silent for a while. But Vasíli Andréevich wished to talk.

'Well, did you tell your wife not to give the cooper any vodka?' he began in the same loud tone, quite convinced that Nikíta must feel flattered to be talking with so clever and important a person as himself, and he was so pleased with his jest that it did not enter his head that the remark might be unpleasant to Nikíta.

The wind again prevented Nikíta's hearing his master's words.

Vasíli Andréevich repeated the jest about the cooper in his loud, clear voice.

'That's their business, Vasíli Andréevich. I don't pry into their affairs. As long as she doesn't ill-treat our boy—God be with them.'

'That's so,' said Vasíli Andréevich. 'Well, and will you be buying a horse in spring?' he went on, changing the subject.

'Yes, I can't avoid it,' answered Nikíta, turning down his collar and leaning back towards his master.

The conversation now became interesting to him and he did not wish to lose a word.

'The lad's growing up. He must begin to plough for himself, but till now we've always had to hire someone,' he said.

'Well, why not have the lean-cruppered one. I won't charge much for it,' shouted Vasíli Andréevich, feeling animated, and consequently starting on his favourite occupation—that of horse-dealing—which absorbed all his mental powers.

'Or you might let me have fifteen rubles and I'll buy one at the horse-market,' said Nikíta, who knew that the horse Vasíli Andréevich wanted to sell him would be dear at seven rubles, but that if he took it from him it would be charged at twenty-five, and then he would be unable to draw any money for half a year.

'It's a good horse. I think of your interest as of my own—according to conscience. Brekhunóv isn't a man to wrong anyone. Let the loss be mine. I'm not like others. Honestly!' he shouted in the voice in which he hypnotized his customers and dealers. 'It's a real good horse.'

'Quite so!' said Nikíta with a sigh, and convinced that there was nothing more to listen to, he again released his collar, which immediately covered his ear and face.

They drove on in silence for about half an hour. The wind blew sharply onto Nikíta's side and arm where his sheepskin was torn.

He huddled up and breathed into the collar which covered his mouth, and was not wholly cold.

'What do you think—shall we go through Karamýshevo or by the straight road?' asked Vasíli Andréevich.

The road through Karamýshevo was more frequented and was well marked with a double row of high stakes. The straight road was nearer but little used and had no stakes, or only poor ones covered with snow.

Nikíta thought awhile.

'Though Karamýshevo is farther, it is better going,' he said.

'But by the straight road, when once we get through the hollow by the forest, it's good going—sheltered,' said Vasíli Andréevich, who wished to go the nearest way.

'Just as you please,' said Nikíta, and again let go of his collar.

Vasíli Andréevich did as he had said, and having gone about half a verst came to a tall oak stake which had a few dry leaves still dangling on it, and there he turned to the left.

On turning they faced directly against the wind, and snow was beginning to fall. Vasíli Andréevich, who was driving, inflated his cheeks, blowing the breath out through his moustache. Nikíta dosed.

So they went on in silence for about ten minutes. Suddenly Vasíli Andréevich began saying something.

'Eh, what?' asked Nikíta, opening his eyes.

Vasíli Andréevich did not answer, but bent over, looking behind them and then ahead of the horse. The sweat had curled Mukhórty's coat between his legs and on his neck. He went at a walk.

'What is it? Nikíta asked again.

'What is it? What is it?' Vasíli Andréevich mimicked him angrily. 'There are no stakes to be seen! We must have got off the road!'

'Well, pull up then, and I'll look for it,' said Nikíta, and jumping down lightly from the sledge and taking the whip from under the straw, he went off to the left from his own side of the sledge.

The snow was not deep that year, so that it was possible to walk anywhere, but still in places it was knee-deep and got into Nikíta's boots. He went about feeling the ground with his feet and the whip, but could not find the road anywhere.

'Well, how is it?' asked Vasíli Andréevich when Nikíta came back to the sledge.

'There is no road this side. I must go to the other side and try there,' said Nikíta.

'There's something there in front. Go and have a look'

Nikíta went to what had appeared dark, but found that it was earth which the wind had blown from the bare fields of winter oats and had strewn over the snow, colouring it. Having searched to the right also, he returned to the sledge, brushed the snow from his coat, shook it out of his boots, and seated himself once more.

'We must go to the right,' he said decidedly. 'The wind was blowing on our left before, but now it is straight in my face. Drive to the right,' he repeated with decision.

Vasíli Andréevich took his advice and turned to the right, but still there was no road. They went on in that direction for some time. The wind was as fierce as ever and it was snowing lightly.

'It seems, Vasíli Andréevich, that we have gone quite astray,' Nikíta suddenly remarked, as if it were a pleasant thing. 'What is that?' he added, pointing to some potato vines that showed up from under the snow

Vasíli Andréevich stopped the perspiring horse, whose deep sides were heaving heavily.

'What is it?'

'Why, we are on the Zakhárov lands. See where we've got to!'

'Nonsense!' retorted Vasíli Andréevich.

'It's not nonsense, Vasíli Andréevich. It's the truth,' replied Nikíta. 'You can feel that the sledge is going over a potato-field, and there are the heaps of vines which have been carted here. It's the Zakhárov factory land.'

'Dear me, how we have gone astray!' said Vasíli Andréevich. 'What are we to do now?'

'We must go straight on, that's all. We shall come out some-where—if not at Zakhárova, then at the proprietor's farm,' said Nikíta.

Vasíli Andréevich agreed, and drove as Nikíta had indicated. So they went on for a considerable time. At times they came onto bare fields and the sledge-runners rattled over frozen lumps of earth. Sometimes they got onto a winter-rye field, or a fallow field on which they could see stalks of wormwood, and straws sticking up through the snow and swaying in the wind; sometimes they came onto deep and even white snow, above which nothing was to be seen.

The snow was falling from above and sometimes rose from below. The horse was evidently exhausted, his hair had all curled up from sweat and was covered with hoarfrost, and he went at a walk. Suddenly he stumbled and sat down in a ditch or water-course. Vasíli Andréevich wanted to stop, but Nikíta cried to him:

'Why stop? We've got in and must get out. Hey, pet! Hey, darling! Gee up, old fellow!' he shouted in a cheerful tone to the horse, jumping out of the sledge and himself getting stuck in the ditch.

The horse gave a start and quickly climbed out onto the frozen bank. It was evidently a ditch that had been dug there.

'Where are we now?' asked Vasíli Andréevich.

'We'll soon find out!' Nikíta replied. 'Go on, we'll get somewhere.'

'Why, this must be the Goryáchkin forest!' said Vasíli Andréevich, pointing to something dark that appeared amid the snow in front of them.

'We'll see what forest it is when we get there,' said Nikíta.

He saw that beside the black thing they had noticed, dry, oblong willow-leaves were fluttering, and so he knew it was not a forest but a settlement, but he did not wish to say so. And in fact they had not gone twenty-five yards beyond the ditch before something in front of them, evidently trees, showed up black, and they heard a new and melancholy sound. Nikíta had guessed right: it was not a wood, but a row of tall willows with a few leaves still fluttering on them here and there. They had evidently been planted along the ditch round a threshing-floor. Coming up to the willows, which moaned sadly in the wind, the horse suddenly planted his forelegs above the height of the sledge, drew up his hind legs also, pulling the sledge onto higher ground, and turned to the left, no longer sinking up to his knees in snow. They were back on a road.

'Well, here we are, but heaven only knows where!' said Nikíta.

The horse kept straight along the road through the drifted snow, and before they had gone another hundred yards the straight line of the dark wattle wall of a barn showed up black before them, its roof heavily covered with snow which poured down from it. After passing the barn the road turned to the wind and they drove into a snow-drift. But ahead of them was a lane with houses on either side, so evidently the snow had been blown across the road and they had to drive through the drift. And so in fact it was. Having driven through the snow they came out into a street. At the end house of the village some frozen clothes hanging on a line—shirts, one red and one white, trousers, leg-bands, and a petticoat—fluttered wildly in the wind. The white shirt in particular struggled desperately, waving its sleeves about.

'There now, either a lazy woman or a dead one has not taken her clothes down before the holiday,' remarked Nikíta, looking at the fluttering shirts.

III

At the entrance to the street the wind still raged and the road was thickly covered with snow, but well within the village it was calm, warm, and cheerful. At one house a dog was barking, at another a woman, covering her head with her coat, came running from somewhere and entered the door of a hut, stopping on the threshold to have a look at the passing sledge. In the middle of the village girls could be heard singing.

Here in the village there seemed to be less wind and snow, and the frost was less keen.

'Why, this is Gríshkino,' said Vasíli Andréevich.

'So it is,' responded Nikíta.

It really was Gríshkino, which meant that they had gone too far to the left and had travelled some six miles, not quite in the direction they aimed at, but towards their destination for all that.

From Gríshkino to Goryáchkin was about another four miles.

In the middle of the village they almost ran into a tall man walking down the middle of the street.

'Who are you?' shouted the man, stopping the horse, and recognizing Vasíli Andréevich he immediately took hold of the shaft, went along it hand over hand till he reached the sledge, and placed himself on the driver's seat.

He was Isáy, a peasant of Vasíli Andréevich's acquaintance, and well known as the principal horse-thief in the district.

'Ah, Vasíli Andréevich! Where are you off to?' said Isáy, enveloping Nikíta in the odour of the vodka he had drunk.

'We were going to Goryáchkin.'

'And look where you've got to! You should have gone through Molchánovka.'

'Should have, but didn't manage it,' said Vasíli Andréevich, holding in the horse.

'That's a good horse,' said Isáy, with a shrewd glance at Mukhórty, and with a practised hand he tightened the loosened knot high in the horse's bushy tail.

'Are you going to stay the night?'

'No, friend. I must get on.'

'Your business must be pressing. And who is this? Ah, Nikíta Stepánych!'

'Who else?' replied Nikíta. 'But I say, good friend, how are we to avoid going astray again?'

'Where can you go astray here? Turn back straight down the street and then when you come out keep straight on. Don't take to the left. You will come out onto the high road, and then turn to the right.'

'And where do we turn off the high road? As in summer, or the winter way?' asked Nikíta.

'The winter way. As soon as you turn off you'll see some bushes, and opposite them there is a way-mark—a large oak, one with branches—and that's the way.'

Vasíli Andréevich turned the horse back and drove through the outskirts of the village.

'Why not stay the night?' Isáy shouted after them.

But Vasíli Andréevich did not answer and touched up the horse. Four miles of good road, two of which lay through the forest, seemed easy to manage, especially as the wind was apparently quieter and the snow had stopped.

Having driven along the trodden village street, darkened here and there by fresh manure, past the yard where the clothes hung out and where the white shirt had broken loose and was now attached only by one frozen sleeve, they again came within sound of the weird moan of the willows, and again emerged on the open fields. The storm, far from ceasing, seemed to have grown yet stronger. The road was completely covered with drifting snow, and only the stakes showed that they had not lost their way. But even the stakes ahead of them were not easy to see, since the wind blew in their faces.

Vasíli Andréevich screwed up his eyes, bent down his head, and looked out for the way-marks, but trusted mainly to the horse's sagacity, letting it take its own way. And the horse really did not lose the road but followed its windings, turning now to the right and now to the left and sensing it under his feet, so that though the snow fell thicker and the wind strengthened they still continued to see way-marks now to the left and now to the right of them.

So they travelled on for about ten minutes, when suddenly, through the slanting screen of wind-driven snow, something black showed up which moved in front of the horse.

This was another sledge with fellow-travellers. Mukhórty overtook them, and struck his hoofs against the back of the sledge in front of him.

'Pass on . . . hey there . . . get in front!' cried voices from the sledge.

Vasíli Andréevich swerved aside to pass the other sledge. In it sat three men and a woman, evidently visitors returning from a feast. One peasant was whacking the snow-covered croup of their little horse with a long switch, and the other two sitting in front waved their arms and shouted something. The woman, completely wrapped up and covered with snow, sat drowsing and bumping at the back.

'Who are you?' shouted Vasíli Andréevich.

'From A-a-a . . .' was all that could be heard.

'I say, where are you from?'

'From A-a-a-a!' one of the peasants shouted with all his might, but still it was impossible to make out who they were.

'Get along! Keep up!' shouted another, ceaselessly beating his horse with the switch.

'So you're from a feast, it seems?'

'Go on, go on! Faster, Simon! Get in front! Faster!'

The wings of the sledges bumped against one another, almost got jammed but managed to separate, and the peasants' sledge began to fall behind.

Their shaggy, big bellied horse, all covered with snow, breathed heavily under the low shaft-bow and, evidently using the last of its strength, vainly endeavoured to escape from the switch, hobbling with its short legs through the deep snow which it threw up under itself.

Its muzzle, young-looking, with the nether lip drawn up like that of a fish, nostrils distended and ears pressed back from fear, kept up for a few seconds near Nikíta's shoulder and then began to fall behind.

'Just see what liquor does!' said Nikíta. 'They've tired that little horse to death. What pagans!'

For a few minutes they heard the panting of the tired little horse and the drunken shouting of the peasants. Then the panting and the shouts died away, and around them nothing could be heard but the whistling of the wind in their ears and now and then the squeak of their sledge-runners over a wind-swept part of the road.

This encounter cheered and enlivened Vasíli Andréevich, and he drove on more boldly without examining the way-marks, urging on the horse and trusting to him.

Nikíta had nothing to do, and as usual in such circumstances he drowsed, making up for much sleepless time. Suddenly the horse stopped and Nikíta nearly fell forward onto his nose.

'You know we're off the track again!' said Vasíli Andréevich.

'How's that?'

'Why, there are no way-marks to be seen. We must have got off the road again.'

'Well, if we've lost the road we must find it,' said Nikíta curtly, and getting out and stepping lightly on his pigeontoed feet he started once more going about on the snow.

He walked about for a long time, now disappearing and now reappearing, and finally he came back.

'There is no road here. There may be farther on,' he said, getting into the sledge.

It was already growing dark. The snow-storm had not increased but had also not subsided.

'If we could only hear those peasants!' said Vasíli Andréevich.

'Well they haven't caught us up. We must have gone far astray. Or maybe they have lost their way too.'

'Where are we to go then?' asked Vasíli Andréevich.

'Why, we must let the horse take its own way,' said Nikíta. 'He will take us right. Let me have the reins.'

Vasíli Andréevich gave him the reins, the more willingly because his hands were beginning to feel frozen in his thick gloves.

Nikíta took the reins, but only held them, trying not to shake them and rejoicing at his favourite's sagacity. And indeed the clever horse, turning first one ear and then the other now to one side and then to the other, began to wheel round.

'The one thing he can't do is to talk,' Nikíta kept saying. 'See what he is doing! Go on, go on! You know best. That's it, that's it!'

The wind was now blowing from behind and it felt warmer.

'Yes, he's clever,' Nikíta continued, admiring the horse. 'A Kirgiz horse is strong but stupid. But this one—just see what he's doing with his ears! He doesn't need any telegraph. He can scent a mile off.'

Before another half-hour had passed they saw something dark ahead of them—a wood or a village—and stakes again appeared to the right They had evidently come out onto the road.

'Why, that's Gríshkino again!' Nikíta suddenly exclaimed.

And indeed, there on their left was that same barn with the snow flying from it, and farther on the same line with the frozen washing, shirts and trousers, which still fluttered desperately in the wind.

Again they drove into the street and again it grew quiet, warm, and cheerful, and again they could see the manure-stained street and hear voices and songs and the barking of a dog. It was already so dark that there were lights in some of the windows.

Half-way through the village Vasíli Andréevich turned the horse towards a large double-fronted brick house and stopped at the porch.

Nikíta went to the lighted snow-covered window, in the rays of which flying snow-flakes glittered, and knocked at it with his whip.

'Who is there?' a voice replied to his knock.

'From Krestý, the Brekhunóvs, dear fellow,' answered Nikíta. 'Just come out for a minute.'

Someone moved from the window, and a minute or two later there was the sound of the passage door as it came unstuck, then the latch of the outside door clicked and a tall white-bearded peasant, with a sheepskin coat thrown over his white holiday shirt, pushed his way out holding the door firmly against the wind, followed by a lad in a red shirt and high leather boots.

'Is that you, Andréevich?' asked the old man.

'Yes, friend, we've gone astray,' said Vasíli Andréevich. 'We wanted to get to Goryáchkin but found ourselves here. We went a second time but lost our way again.'

'Just see how you have gone astray!' said the old man. 'Petrúshka, go and open the gate!' he added, turning to the lad in the red shirt.

'All right,' said the lad in a cheerful voice, and ran back into the passage.

'But we're not staying the night,' said Vasíli Andréevich.

'Where will you go in the night? You'd better stay!'

'I'd be glad to, but I must go on. It's business, and it can't be helped.'

'Well, warm yourself at least. The samovar is just ready.'

'Warm myself? Yes, I'll do that,' said Vasíli Andréevich. 'It won't get darker. The moon will rise and it will be lighter. Let's go in and warm ourselves, Nikíta.'

'Well, why not? Let us warm ourselves,' replied Nikíta, who was stiff with cold and anxious to warm his frozen limbs.

Vasíli Andréevich went into the room with the old man, and Nikíta drove through the gate opened for him by Petrúshka, by whose advice he backed the horse under the penthouse. The ground was covered with manure and the tall bow over the horse's head caught against the beam. The hens and the cock had already settled to roost there, and clucked peevishly, clinging to the beam with their claws. The disturbed sheep shied and rushed aside trampling the frozen manure with their hooves. The dog yelped desperately with fright and anger and then burst out barking like a puppy at the stranger.

Nikíta talked to them all, excused himself to the fowls and assured them that he would not disturb them again, rebuked the sheep for being frightened without knowing why, and kept soothing the dog, while he tied up the horse.

'Now that will be all right,' he said, knocking the snow off his clothes. 'Just hear how he barks!' he added, turning to the dog. 'Be quiet, stupid! Be quiet. You are only troubling yourself for nothing. We're not thieves, we're friends. . . .'

'And these are, it's said, the three domestic counsellors,' remarked the lad, and with his strong arms he pushed under the pent-roof the sledge that had remained outside.

'Why counsellors?' asked Nikíta.

'That's what is printed in Paulson. A thief creeps to a house—the dog barks, that means, "Be on your guard!" The cock crows, that means, "Get up!" The cat licks herself—that means, "A welcome guest is coming. Get ready to receive him!"' said the lad with a smile.

Petrúshka could read and write and knew Paulson's primer, his only book, almost by heart, and he was fond of quoting sayings from it that he thought suited the occasion, especially when he had had something to drink, as to-day.

'That's so,' said Nikíta.

'You must be chilled through and through,' said Petrúshka.

'Yes, I am rather,' said Nikíta, and they went across the yard and the passage into the house.

IV

The household to which Vasíli Andréevich had come was one of the richest in the village. The family had five allotments, besides renting other land. They had six horses, three cows, two calves, and some twenty sheep. There were twenty-two members belonging to the homestead: four married sons, six grandchildren (one of whom, Petrúshka, was married), two great-grandchildren, three orphans, and four daughters-in-law with their babies. It was one of the few homesteads that remained still undivided, but even here the dull internal work of disintegration which would inevitably lead to separation had already begun, starting as usual among the women. Two sons were living in Moscow as water-carriers, and one was in the army. At home now were the old man and his wife, their second son who managed the homestead, the eldest who had come from Moscow for the holiday, and all the women and children. Besides these members of the family there was a visitor, a neighbour who was godfather to one of the children.

Over the table in the room hung a lamp with a shade, which brightly lit up the tea-things, a bottle of vodka, and some refreshments, besides illuminating the brick walls, which in the far corner were hung with icons on both sides of which were pictures. At the head of the table sat Vasíli Andréevich in a black sheepskin coat, sucking his frozen moustache and observing the room and the people around him with his prominent hawk-like eyes. With him sat the old, bald, white-bearded master of the house in a white homespun shirt, and next him the son home from Moscow for the holiday—a man with a sturdy back and powerful shoulders and clad in a thin print shirt—then the second son, also broad-shouldered, who acted as head of the house, and then a lean red-haired peasant—the neighbour.

Having had a drink of vodka and something to eat, they were about to take tea, and the samovar standing on the floor beside the brick oven was already humming. The children could be seen in the top bunks and on the top of the oven. A woman sat on a lower bunk with a cradle beside her. The old housewife, her face covered with wrinkles which wrinkled even her lips, was waiting on Vasíli Andréevich.

As Nikíta entered the house she was offering her guest a small tumbler of thick glass which she had just filled with vodka.

'Don't refuse, Vasíli Andréevich, you mustn't! Wish us a merry feast. Drink it, dear!' she said.

The sight and smell of vodka, especially now when he was chilled through and tired out, much disturbed Nikíta's mind. He frowned, and having shaken the snow off his cap and coat, stopped in front of the icons as if not seeing anyone, crossed himself three times, and bowed to the icons. Then, turning to the old master of the house and bowing first to him, then to all those at table, then to the women who stood by the oven, and muttering: 'A merry holiday!' he began taking off his outer things without looking at the table.

'Why, you're all covered with hoar-frost, old fellow!' said the eldest brother, looking at Nikíta's snow-covered face, eyes, and beard.

Nikíta took off his coat, shook it again, hung it up beside the oven, and came up to the table. He too was offered vodka. He went through a moment of painful hesitation and nearly took up the glass and emptied the clear fragrant liquid down his throat, but he glanced at Vasíli Andréevich, remembered his oath and the boots that he had sold for drink, recalled the cooper, remembered his son for whom he had promised to buy a horse by spring, sighed, and declined it.

'I don't drink, thank you kindly,' he said frowning, and sat down on a bench near the second window.

'How's that?' asked the eldest brother.

'I just don't drink,' replied Nikíta without lifting his eyes but looking askance at his scanty beard and moustache and getting the icicles out of them.

'It's not good for him,' said Vasíli Andréevich, munching a cracknel after emptying his glass.

'Well, then, have some tea,' said the kindly old hostess. 'You must be chilled through, good soul. Why are you women dawdling so with the samovar?'

'It is ready,' said one of the young women, and after flicking with her apron the top of the samovar which was now boiling over, she carried it with an effort to the table, raised it, and set it down with a thud.

Meanwhile Vasíli Andréevich was telling how he had lost his way, how they had come back twice to this same village, and how they had gone astray and had met some drunken peasants. Their hosts were surprised, explained where and why they had missed their way, said who the tipsy people they had met were, and told them how they ought to go.

'A little child could find the way to Molchánovka from here. All you have to do is to take the right turning from the high road. There's a bush you can see just there. But you didn't even get that far!' said the neighbour.

'You'd better stay the night. The women will make up beds for you,' said the old woman persuasively.

'You could go on in the morning and it would be pleasanter,' said the old man, confirming what his wife had said.

'I can't, friend. Business!' said Vasíli Andréevich. 'Lose an hour and you can't catch it up in a year,' he added, remembering the grove and the dealers who might snatch that deal from him. 'We shall get there, shan't we?' he said, turning to Nikíta.

Nikíta did not answer for some time, apparently still intent on thawing out his beard and moustache.

'If only we don't go astray again,' he replied gloomily.

He was gloomy because he passionately longed for some vodka, and the only thing that could assuage that longing was tea and he had not yet been offered any.

'But we have only to reach the turning and then we shan't go wrong. The road will be through the forest the whole way,' said Vasíli Andréevich.

'It's just as you please, Vasíli Andréevich. If we're to go, let us go,' said Nikíta, taking the glass of tea he was offered.

'We'll drink our tea and be off.'

Nikíta said nothing but only shook his head, and carefully pouring some tea into his saucer began warming his hands, the fingers of which were always swollen with hard work, over the steam. Then, biting off a tiny bit of sugar, he bowed to his hosts, said, 'Your health!' and drew in the steaming liquid.

'If somebody would see us as far as the turning,' said Vasíli Andréevich.

'Well, we can do that,' said the eldest son. 'Petrúshka will harness and go that far with you.'

'Well, then, put in the horse, lad, and I shall be thankful to you for it.'

'Oh, what for, dear man?' said the kindly old woman. 'We are heartily glad to do it.'

'Petrúshka, go and put in the mare,' said the eldest brother.

'All right,' replied Petrúshka with a smile, and promptly snatching his cap down from a nail he ran away to harness.

While the horse was being harnessed the talk returned to the point at which it had stopped when Vasíli Andréevich drove up to the window. The old man had been complaining to his neighbour, the village elder, about his third son who had not sent him anything for the holiday though he had sent a French shawl to his wife.

'The young people are getting out of hand,' said the old man.

'And how they do!' said the neighbour. 'There's no managing them! They know too much. There's Demóchkin now, who broke his father's arm. It's all from being too clever, it seems.'

Nikíta listened, watched their faces, and evidently would have liked to share in the conversation, but he was too busy drinking his tea and only nodded his head approvingly. He emptied one tumbler after another and grew warmer and warmer and more and more comfortable. The talk continued on the same subject for a long time—the harmfulness of a household dividing up—and it was clearly not an abstract discussion but concerned the question of a separation in that house; a separation demanded by the second son who sat there morosely silent.

It was evidently a sore subject and absorbed them all, but out of propriety they did not discuss their private affairs before strangers. At last, however, the old man could not restrain himself, and with tears in his eyes declared that he would not consent to a break-up of the family during his lifetime, that his house was prospering, thank God, but that if they separated they would all have to go begging.

'Just like the Matvéevs,' said the neighbour. 'They used to have a proper house, but now they've split up none of them has anything.'

'And that is what you want to happen to us,' said the old man, turning to his son.

The son made no reply and there was an awkward pause. The silence was broken by Petrúshka, who having harnessed the horse had returned to the hut a few minutes before this and had been listening all the time with a smile.

'There's a fable about that in Paulson,' he said. 'A father gave his sons a broom to break. At first they could not break it, but when they took it twig by twig they broke it easily. And it's the same here,' and he gave a broad smile. 'I'm ready!' he added.

'If you're ready, let's go,' said Vasíli Andréevich. 'And as to separating, don't you allow it, Grandfather. You got everything together and you're the master. Go to the Justice of the Peace. He'll say how things should be done.'

'He carries on so, carries on so,' the old man continued in a whining tone. 'There's no doing anything with him. It's as if the devil possessed him.'

Nikíta having meanwhile finished his fifth tumbler of tea laid it on its side instead of turning it upside down, hoping to be offered a sixth glass. But there was no more water in the samovar, so the hostess did not fill it up for him. Besides, Vasíli Andréevich was putting his things on, so there was nothing for it but for Nikíta to get up too, put back into the sugar-basin the lump of sugar he had nibbled all round, wipe his perspiring face with the skirt of his sheepskin, and go to put on his overcoat.

Having put it on he sighed deeply, thanked his hosts, said good-bye, and went out of the warm bright room into the cold dark passage, through which the wind was howling and where snow was blowing through the cracks of the shaking door, and from there into the yard.

Petrúshka stood in his sheepskin in the middle of the yard by his horse, repeating some lines from Paulson's primer. He said with a smile:

> '*Storms with mist the sky conceal,*
> *Snowy circles wheeling wild.*
> *Now like savage beast 'twill howl,*
> *And now 'tis wailing like a child.*'

Nikíta nodded approvingly as he arranged the reins.

The old man, seeing Vasíli Andréevich off, brought a lantern into the passage to show him a light, but it was blown out at once. And even in the yard it was evident that the snowstorm had become more violent.

'Well, this is weather!' thought Vasíli Andréevich. 'Perhaps we may not get there after all. But there is nothing to be done. Business! Besides, we have got ready, our host's horse has been harnessed, and we'll get there with God's help!'

Their aged host also thought they ought not to go, but he had already tried to persuade them to stay and had not been listened to.

'It's no use asking them again. Maybe my age makes me timid. They'll get there all right, and at least we shall get to bed in good time and without any fuss,' he thought.

Petrúshka did not think of danger. He knew the road and the whole district so well, and the lines about 'snowy circles wheeling wild' described what was happening outside so aptly that it cheered him up. Nikíta did not wish to go at all, but he had been accustomed not to have his own way and to serve others for so long that there was no one to hinder the departing travellers.

V

Vasíli Andréevich went over to his sledge, found it with difficulty in the darkness, climbed in and took the reins.

'Go on in front!' he cried.

Petrúshka kneeling in his low sledge started his horse. Mukhórty, who had been neighing for some time past, now scenting a mare ahead of him started after her, and they drove out into the street. They drove again through the outskirts of the village and along the same road, past the yard where the frozen linen had hung (which, however, was no longer to be seen), past the same barn, which was now snowed up almost to the roof and from which the snow was still endlessly pouring, past the same dismally moaning, whistling, and swaying willows, and again entered into the sea of blustering snow raging from above and below. The wind was so strong that when it blew from the side and the travellers steered against it, it tilted the sledges and turned the horses to one side. Petrúshka drove his good mare in front at a brisk trot and kept shouting lustily. Mukhórty pressed after her.

After travelling so for about ten minutes, Petrúshka turned round and shouted something. Neither Vasíli Andréevich nor Nikíta could hear anything because of the wind, but they guessed that they had arrived at the turning. In fact Petrúshka had turned to the right, and now the wind that had blown from the side blew straight in their faces, and through the snow they saw something dark on their right. It was the bush at the turning.

'Well now, God speed you!'

'Thank you, Petrúshka!'

'Storms with mist the sky conceal!' shouted Petrúshka as he disappeared.

'There's a poet for you!' muttered Vasíli Andréevich, pulling at the reins.

'Yes, a fine lad—a true peasant,' said Nikíta.

They drove on.

Nikíta, wrapping his coat closely about him and pressing his head down so close to his shoulders that his short beard covered his throat, sat silently, trying not to lose the warmth he had obtained while drinking tea in the house. Before him he saw the straight lines of the shafts which constantly deceived him into thinking they were on a well-travelled road, and the horse's swaying crupper with his knotted tail blown to one side, and farther ahead the high shaft-bow and the swaying head and neck of the horse with its waving mane. Now and then he caught sight of a way-sign, so that he knew they were still on a road and that there was nothing for him to be concerned about.

Vasíli Andréevich drove on, leaving it to the horse to keep to the road. But Mukhórty, though he had had a breathing-space in the village, ran reluctantly, and seemed now and then to get off the road, so that Vasíli Andréevich had repeatedly to correct him.

'Here's a stake to the right, and another, and here's a third,' Vasíli Andréevich counted, 'and here in front is the forest,' thought he, as he looked at something dark in front of him. But what had seemed to him a forest was only a bush. They passed the bush and drove on for another hundred yards but there was no fourth way-mark nor any forest.

'We must reach the forest soon,' thought Vasíli Andréevich, and animated by the vodka and the tea he did not stop but shook the reins, and the good obedient horse responded, now ambling, now slowly trotting in the direction in which he was sent, though he knew that he was not going the right way. Ten minutes went by, but there was still no forest.

'There now, we must be astray again,' said Vasíli Andréevich, pulling up.

Nikíta silently got out of the sledge and holding his coat, which the wind now wrapped closely about him and now almost tore off, started to feel about in the snow, going first to one side and then to the other. Three or four times he was completely lost to sight. At last he returned and took the reins from Vasíli Andréevich's hand.

'We must go to the right,' he said sternly and peremptorily, as he turned the horse.

'Well, if it's to the right, go to the right,' said Vasíli Andréevich, yielding up the reins to Nikíta and thrusting his freezing hands into his sleeves.

Nikíta did not reply.

'Now then, friend, stir yourself!' he shouted to the horse, but in spite of the shake of the reins Mukhórty moved only at a walk.

The snow in places was up to his knees, and the sledge moved by fits and starts with his every movement.

Nikíta took the whip that hung over the front of the sledge and struck him once. The good horse, unused to the whip, sprang forward and moved at a trot, but immediately fell back into an amble and then to a walk. So they went on for five minutes. It was dark and the snow whirled from above and rose from below, so that sometimes the shaft-bow could not be seen. At times the sledge seemed to stand still and the field to run backwards. Suddenly the horse stopped abruptly, evidently aware of something close in front of him. Nikíta again sprang lightly out, throwing down the reins, and went ahead to see what had brought him to a standstill, but hardly had he made a step in front of the horse before his feet slipped and he went rolling down an incline.

'Whoa, whoa, whoa!' he said to himself as he fell, and he tried to stop his fall but could not, and only stopped when his feet plunged into a thick layer of snow that had drifted to the bottom of the hollow.

The fringe of a drift of snow that hung on the edge of the hollow, disturbed by Nikíta's fall, showered down on him and got inside his collar.

'What a thing to do!' said Nikíta reproachfully, addressing the drift and the hollow and shaking the snow from under his collar.

'Nikíta! Hey, Nikíta!' shouted Vasíli Andréevich from above.

But Nikíta did not reply. He was too occupied in shaking out the snow and searching for the whip he had dropped when rolling down the incline. Having found the whip he tried to climb straight up the bank where he had rolled down, but it was impossible to do so: he kept rolling down again, and so he had to go along at the foot of the hollow to find a way up. About seven yards farther on he managed with difficulty to crawl up the incline on all fours, then he followed the edge of the hollow back to the place where the horse should have been. He could not see either horse or sledge, but as he walked against the wind he heard Vasíli Andréevich's shouts and Mukhórty's neighing, calling him.

'I'm coming! I'm coming! What are you cackling for?' he muttered.

Only when he had come up to the sledge could he make out the horse, and Vasíli Andréevich standing beside it and looking gigantic.

'Where the devil did you vanish to? We must go back, if only to Gríshkino,' he began reproaching Nikíta.

'I'd be glad to get back, Vasíli Andréevich, but which way are we to go? There is such a ravine here that if we once get in it we shan't get out again. I got stuck so fast there myself that I could hardly get out.'

'What shall we do, then? We can't stay here! We must go somewhere!' said Vasíli Andréevich.

Nikíta said nothing. He seated himself in the sledge with his back to the wind, took off his boots, shook out the snow that had got into them, and taking some straw from the bottom of the sledge, carefully plugged with it a hole in his left boot.

Vasíli Andréevich remained silent, as though now leaving everything to Nikíta. Having put his boots on again, Nikíta drew his feet into the sledge, put on his mittens and took up the reins, and directed the horse along the side of the ravine. But they had not gone a hundred yards before the horse again stopped short. The ravine was in front of him again.

Nikíta again climbed out and again trudged about in the snow. He did this for a considerable time and at last appeared from the opposite side to that from which he had started.

'Vasíli Andréevich, are you alive?' he called out.

'Here!' replied Vasíli Andréevich. 'Well, what now?'

'I can't make anything out. It's too dark. There's nothing but ravines. We must drive against the wind again.'

They set off once more. Again Nikíta went stumbling through the snow, again he fell in, again climbed out and trudged about, and at last quite out of breath he sat down beside the sledge.

'Well, how now?' asked Vasíli Andréevich.

'Why, I am quite worn out and the horse won't go.'

'Then what's to be done?'

'Why, wait a minute.'

Nikíta went away again but soon returned.

'Follow me!' he said, going in front of the horse.

Vasíli Andréevich no longer gave orders but implicitly did what Nikíta told him.

'Here, follow me!' Nikíta shouted, stepping quickly to the right, and seizing the rein he led Mukhórty down towards a snow-drift.

At first the horse held back, then he jerked forward, hoping to leap the drift, but he had not the strength and sank into it up to his collar.

'Get out!' Nikíta called to Vasíli Andréevich who still sat in the sledge, and taking hold of one shaft he moved the sledge closer to the horse. 'It's hard, brother!' he said to Mukhórty, 'but it can't be helped. Make an effort! Now, now, just a little one!' he shouted.

The horse gave a tug, then another, but failed to clear himself and settled down again as if considering something.

'Now, brother, this won't do!' Nikíta admonished him. 'Now once more!'

Again Nikíta tugged at the shaft on his side, and Vasíli Andréevich did the same on the other.

Mukhórty lifted his head and then gave a sudden jerk.

'That's it! That's it!' cried Nikíta. 'Don't be afraid—you won't sink!'

One plunge, another, and a third, and at last Mukhórty was out of the snow-drift, and stood still, breathing heavily and shaking the snow off himself. Nikíta wished to lead him farther, but Vasíli Andréevich, in his two fur coats, was so out of breath that he could not walk farther and dropped into the sledge.

'Let me get my breath!' he said, unfastening the kerchief with which he had tied the collar of his fur coat at the village.

'It's all right here. You lie there,' said Nikíta. 'I will lead him along.' And with Vasíli Andréevich in the sledge he led the horse by the bridle about ten paces down and then up a slight rise, and stopped.

The place where Nikíta had stopped was not completely in the hollow where the snow sweeping down from the hillocks might have buried them altogether, but still it was partly sheltered from the wind by the side of the ravine. There were moments when the wind seemed to abate a little, but that did not last long and as if to make up for that respite the storm swept down with tenfold vigour and tore and whirled the more fiercely. Such a gust struck them at the moment when Vasíli Andréevich, having recovered his breath, got out of the sledge and went up to Nikíta to consult him as to what they should do. They both bent down involuntarily and waited till the violence of the squall should have passed. Mukhórty too laid back his ears and shook his head discontentedly. As soon as the violence of the blast had abated a little, Nikíta took off his mittens, stuck them into his belt, breathed onto his hands, and began to undo the straps of the shaft-bow.

'What's that you are doing there?' asked Vasíli Andréevich.

'Unharnessing. What else is there to do? I have no strength left,' said Nikíta as though excusing himself.

'Can't we drive somewhere?'

'No, we can't. We shall only kill the horse. Why, the poor beast is not himself now,' said Nikíta, pointing to the horse, which was standing submissively waiting for what might come, with his steep wet sides heaving heavily. 'We shall have to stay the night here,' he said, as if preparing to spend the night at an inn, and he proceeded to unfasten the collar-straps. The buckles came undone.

'But shan't we be frozen?' remarked Vasíli Andréevich.

'Well, if we are we can't help it,' said Nikíta.

VI

Although Vasíli Andréevich felt quite warm in his two fur coats, especially after struggling in the snow-drift, a cold shiver ran down his back on realizing that he must really spend the night where they were. To calm himself he sat down in the sledge and got out his cigarettes and matches.

Nikíta meanwhile unharnessed Mukhórty. He unstrapped the belly-band and the back-band, took away the reins, loosened the collar-strap, and removed the shaft-bow, talking to him all the time to encourage him.

'Now come out! come out!' he said, leading him clear of the shafts. 'Now we'll tie you up here and I'll put down some straw and take off your bridle. When you've had a bite you'll feel more cheerful.'

But Mukhórty was restless and evidently not comforted by Nikíta's remarks. He stepped now on one foot and now on another, and pressed close against the sledge, turning his back to the wind and rubbing his head on Nikíta's sleeve. Then, as if not to pain Nikíta by refusing his offer of the straw he put before him, he hurriedly snatched a wisp out of the sledge, but immediately decided that it was now no time to think of straw and threw it down, and the wind instantly scattered it, carried it away, and covered it with snow.

'Now we will set up a signal,' said Nikíta, and turning the front of the sledge to the wind he tied the shafts together with a strap and set them up on end in front of the sledge. 'There now, when the snow covers us up, good folk will see the shafts and dig us out,' he said, slapping his mittens together and putting them on. 'That's what the old folk taught us!'

Vasíli Andréevich meanwhile had unfastened his coat, and holding its skirts up for shelter, struck one sulphur match after another on the steel box. But his hands trembled, and one match after another either did not kindle or was blown out by the wind just as he was lifting it to the cigarette. At last a match did burn up, and its flame lit up for a moment the fur of his coat, his hand with the gold ring on the bent forefinger, and the snow-sprinkled oat-straw that stuck out from under the drugget. The cigarette lighted, he eagerly took a whiff or two, inhaled the smoke, let it out through his moustache, and would have inhaled again, but the wind tore off the burning tobacco and whirled it away as it had done the straw.

But even these few puffs had cheered him.

'If we must spend the night here, we must!' he said with decision. 'Wait a bit, I'll arrange a flag as well,' he added, picking up the kerchief which he had thrown down in the sledge after taking it from round his collar, and drawing off his gloves and standing up on the front of the sledge and stretching himself to reach the strap, he tied the handkerchief to it with a tight knot.

The kerchief immediately began to flutter wildly, now clinging round the shaft, now suddenly streaming out, stretching and flapping.

'Just see what a fine flag!' said Vasíli Andréevich, admiring his handiwork and letting himself down into the sledge. 'We should be warmer together, but there's not room enough for two,' he added.

'I'll find a place,' said Nikíta. 'But I must cover up the horse first—he sweated so, poor thing. Let go!' he added, drawing the drugget from under Vasíli Andréevich.

Having got the drugget he folded it in two, and after taking off the breechband and pad, covered Mukhórty with it.

'Anyhow it will be warmer, silly!' he said, putting back the breechband and the pad on the horse over the drugget. Then having finished that business he returned to the sledge, and addressing Vasíli Andréevich, said: 'You won't need the sackcloth, will you? And let me have some straw.'

And having taken these things from under Vasíli Andréevich, Nikíta went behind the sledge, dug out a hole for himself in the snow, put straw into it, wrapped his coat well round him, covered himself with the sackcloth, and pulling his cap well down seated himself on the straw he had spread, and leant against the wooden back of the sledge to shelter himself from the wind and the snow.

Vasíli Andréevich shook his head disapprovingly at what Nikíta was doing, as in general he disapproved of the peasant's stupidity and lack of education, and he began to settle himself down for the night.

He smoothed the remaining straw over the bottom of the sledge, putting more of it under his side. Then he thrust his hands into his sleeves and settled down, sheltering his head in the corner of the sledge from the wind in front.

He did not wish to sleep. He lay and thought: thought ever of the one thing that constituted the sole aim, meaning, pleasure, and pride of his life—of how much money he had made and might still make, of how much other people he knew had made and possessed, and of how those others had made and were making it, and how he, like them, might still make much more. The purchase of the Goryáchkin grove was a matter of immense importance to him. By that one deal he hoped to make perhaps ten thousand rubles. He began mentally to reckon the value of the wood he had inspected in autumn, and on five acres of which he had counted all the trees.

'The oaks will go for sledge-runners. The undergrowth will take care of itself, and there'll still be some thirty sázheens of fire-wood left on each desyatía,' said he to himself. 'That means there will be at least two hundred and twenty-five rubles' worth left on each desyatía. Fifty-six desyatíns means fifty-six hundreds, and fifty-six hundreds, and fifty-six tens, and another fifty-six tens, and then fifty-six fives. . . .' He saw that it came out to more than twelve thousand rubles, but could not reckon it up exactly without a counting-frame. 'But I won't give ten thousand, anyhow. I'll give about eight thousand with a deduction on account of the glades. I'll grease the surveyor's palm—give him a hundred rubles, or a hundred and fifty, and he'll reckon that there are some five desyatíns of glade to be deducted. And he'll let it go for eight thousand. Three thousand cash down. That'll move him, no fear!' he thought, and he pressed his pocket-book with his forearm.

'God only knows how we missed the turning. The forest ought to be there, and a watchman's hut, and dogs barking. But the damned things don't bark when they're wanted.' He turned his collar down from his ear and listened, but as before only the whistling of the wind could be heard, the flapping and fluttering of the kerchief tied to the shafts, and the pelting of the snow against the woodwork of the sledge. He again covered up his ear.

'If I had known I would have stayed the night. Well, no matter, we'll get there tomorrow. It's only one day lost. And the others won't travel in such weather.' Then he remembered that on the 9th he had to receive payment from the butcher for his oxen. 'He meant to come himself, but he won't find me, and my wife won't know how to receive the money. She doesn't know the right way of doing things,' he thought, recalling how at their party the day before she had not known how to treat the police-officer who was their guest. 'Of course she's only a woman! Where could she have seen anything? In my father's time what was our house like? Just a rich peasant's house: just an oatmill and an inn—that was the whole property. But what have I done in these fifteen years? A shop, two taverns, a flour-mill, a grain-store, two farms leased out, and a house with an iron-roofed barn,' he thought proudly. 'Not as it was in Father's time! Who is talked of in the whole district now? Brekhunóv! And why? Because I stick to business. I take trouble, not like others who lie abed or waste their time on foolishness while I don't sleep of nights. Blizzard or no blizzard I start out. So business gets done. They think money-making is a joke. No, take pains and rack your brains! You get overtaken out of doors at night, like this, or keep awake night after night till the thoughts whirling in your head make the pillow turn,' he meditated with pride. 'They think people get on through luck. After all, the Mirónovs are now millionaires. And why? Take pains and God gives. If only He grants me health!'

The thought that he might himself be a millionaire like Mirónov, who began with nothing, so excited Vasíli Andréevich that he felt the need of talking to somebody. But there was no one to talk to. . . . If only he could have reached Goryáchkin he would have talked to the landlord and shown him a thing or two.

'Just see how it blows! It will snow us up so deep that we shan't be able to get out in the morning!' he thought, listening to a gust of wind that blew against the front of the sledge, bending it and lashing the snow against it. He raised himself and looked round. All he could see through the whirling darkness was Mukhórty's dark head, his back covered by the fluttering drugget, and his thick knotted tail; while all round, in front and behind, was the same fluctuating whity darkness, sometimes seeming to get a little lighter and sometimes growing denser still.

'A pity I listened to Nikíta,' he thought. 'We ought to have driven on. We should have come out somewhere, if only back to Gríshkino and stayed the night at Tarás's. As it is we must sit here all night. But what was I thinking about? Yes, that God gives to those who take trouble, but not to loafers, lie-abeds, or fools. I must have a smoke!'

He sat down again, got out his cigarette-case, and stretched himself flat on his stomach, screening the matches with the skirt of his coat. But the wind found its way in and put out match after match. At last he got one to burn and lit a cigarette. He was very glad that he had managed to do what he wanted, and though the wind smoked more of the cigarette than he did, he still got two or three puffs and felt more cheerful. He again leant back, wrapped himself up, started reflecting and remembering, and suddenly and quite unexpectedly lost consciousness and fell asleep.

Suddenly something seemed to give him a push and awoke him. Whether it was Mukhórty who had pulled some straw from under him, or whether something within him had startled him, at all events it woke him, and his heart began to beat faster and faster so that the sledge seemed to tremble under him. He opened his eyes. Everything around him was just as before. 'It looks lighter,' he thought. 'I expect it won't be long before dawn.' But he at once remembered that it was lighter because the moon had risen. He sat up and looked first at the horse. Mukhórty still stood with his back to the wind, shivering all over. One side of the drugget, which was completely covered with snow, had been blown back, the breeching had slipped down and the snow-covered head with its waving forelock and mane were now more visible. Vasíli Andréevich leant over the back of the sledge and looked behind. Nikíta still sat in the same position in which he had settled himself. The sacking with which he was covered, and his legs, were thickly covered with snow.

'If only that peasant doesn't freeze to death! His clothes are so wretched. I may be held responsible for him. What shiftless people they are—such a want of education,' thought Vasíli Andréevich, and he felt like taking the drugget off the horse and putting it over Nikíta, but it would be very cold to get out and move about and, moreover, the horse might freeze to death. 'Why did I bring him with me? It was all her stupidity!' he thought, recalling his unloved wife, and he rolled over into his old place at the front part of the sledge. 'My uncle once spent a whole night like this,' he reflected, 'and was all right.' But another case came at once to his mind. 'But when they dug Sebastian out he was dead—stiff like a frozen carcass. If I'd only stopped the night in Gríshkino all this would not have happened!'

And wrapping his coat carefully round him so that none of the warmth of the fur should be wasted but should warm him all over, neck, knees, and feet, he shut his eyes and tried to sleep again. But try as he would he could not get drowsy, on the contrary he felt wide awake and animated. Again he began counting his gains and the debts due to him, again he began bragging to himself and feeling pleased with himself and his position, but all this was continually disturbed by a stealthily approaching fear and by the unpleasant regret that he had not remained in Gríshkino.

'How different it would be to be lying warm on a bench!' He turned over several times in his attempts to get into a more comfortable position more sheltered from the wind, he wrapped up his legs closer, shut his eyes, and lay still. But either his legs in their strong felt boots began to ache from being bent in one position, or the wind blew in somewhere, and after lying still for a short time he again began to recall the disturbing fact that he might now have been lying quietly in the warm hut at Gríshkino. He again sat up, turned about, muffled himself up, and settled down once more.

Once he fancied that he heard a distant cock-crow. He felt glad, turned down his coat-collar and listened with strained attention, but in spite of all his efforts nothing could be heard but the wind whistling between the shafts, the flapping of the kerchief, and the snow pelting against the frame of the sledge.

Nikíta sat just as he had done all the time, not moving and not even answering Vasíli Andréevich who had addressed him a couple of times. 'He doesn't care a bit—he's probably asleep!' thought Vasíli Andréevich with vexation, looking behind the sledge at Nikíta who was covered with a thick layer of snow.

Vasíli Andréevich got up and lay down again some twenty times. It seemed to him that the night would never end. 'It must be getting near morning,' he thought, getting up and looking around. 'Let's have a look at my watch. It will be cold to unbutton, but if I only know that it's getting near morning I shall at any rate feel more cheerful. We could begin harnessing.'

In the depth of his heart Vasíli Andréevich knew that it could not yet be near morning, but he was growing more and more afraid, and wished both to get to know and yet to deceive himself. He carefully undid the fastening of his sheepskin, pushed in his hand, and felt about for a long time before he got to his waistcoat. With great difficulty he managed to draw out his silver watch with its enamelled flower design, and tried to make out the time. He could not see anything without a light. Again he went down on his knees and elbows as he had done when he lighted a cigarette, got out his matches, and proceeded to strike one. This time he went to work more carefully, and feeling with his fingers for a match with the largest head and the greatest amount of phosphorus, lit it at the first try. Bringing the face of the watch under the light he could hardly believe his eyes. . . . It was only ten minutes past twelve. Almost the whole night was still before him.

'Oh, how long the night is!' he thought, feeling a cold shudder run down his back, and having fastened his fur coats again and wrapped himself up, he snuggled into a corner of the sledge intending to wait patiently. Suddenly, above the monotonous roar of the wind, he clearly distinguished another new and living sound. It steadily strengthened, and having become quite clear diminished just as gradually. Beyond all doubt it was a wolf, and he was so near that the movement of his jaws as he changed his cry was brought down the wind. Vasíli Andréevich turned back the collar of his coat and listened attentively. Mukhórty too strained to listen, moving his ears, and when the wolf had ceased its howling he shifted from foot to foot and gave a warning snort. After this Vasíli Andréevich could not fall asleep again or even calm himself. The more he tried to think of his accounts, his business, his reputation, his worth and his wealth, the more and more was he mastered by fear, and regrets that he had not stayed the night at Gríshkino dominated and mingled in all his thoughts.

'Devil take the forest! Things were all right without it, thank God. Ah, if we had only put up for the night!' he said to himself. 'They say it's drunkards that freeze,' he thought, 'and I have had some drink.' And observing his sensations he noticed that he was beginning to shiver, without knowing whether it was from cold or from fear. He tried to wrap himself up and lie down as before, but could no longer do so. He could not stay in one position. He wanted to get up, to do something to master the gathering fear that was rising in him and against which he felt himself powerless. He again got out his cigarettes and matches, but only three matches were left and they were bad ones. The phosphorus rubbed off them all without lighting.

'The devil take you! Damned thing! Curse you!' he muttered, not knowing whom or what he was cursing, and he flung away the crushed cigarette. He was about to throw away the matchbox too, but checked the movement of his hand and put the box in his pocket instead. He was seized with such unrest that he could no longer remain in one spot. He climbed out of the sledge and standing with his back to the wind began to shift his belt again, fastening it lower down in the waist and tightening it.

'What's the use of lying and waiting for death? Better mount the horse and get away!' The thought suddenly occurred to him. 'The horse will move when he has someone on his back. As for him,' he thought of Nikíta—'it's all the same to him whether he lives or dies. What is his life worth? He won't grudge his life, but I have something to live for, thank God.'

He untied the horse, threw the reins over his neck and tried to mount, but his coats and boots were so heavy that he failed. Then he clambered up in the sledge and tried to mount from there, but the sledge tilted under his weight, and he failed again. At last he drew Mukhórty nearer to the sledge, cautiously balanced on one side of it, and managed to lie on his stomach across the horse's back. After lying like that for a while he shifted forward once and again, threw a leg over, and finally seated himself, supporting his feet on the loose breeching-straps. The shaking of the sledge awoke Nikíta. He raised himself, and it seemed to Vasíli Andréevich that he said something.

'Listen to such fools as you! Am I to die like this for nothing?' exclaimed Vasíli Andréevich. And tucking the loose skirts of his fur coat in under his knees, he turned the horse and rode away from the sledge in the direction in which he thought the forest and the forester's hut must be.

VII

From the time he had covered himself with the sackcloth and seated himself behind the sledge, Nikíta had not stirred. Like all those who live in touch with nature and have known want, he was patient and could wait for hours, even days, without growing restless or irritable. He heard his master call him, but did not answer because he did not want to move or talk. Though he still felt some warmth from the tea he had drunk and from his energetic struggle when clambering about in the snowdrift, he knew that this warmth would not last long and that he had no strength left to warm himself again by moving about, for he felt as tired as a horse when it stops and refuses to go further in spite of the whip, and its master sees that it must be fed before it can work again. The foot in the boot with a hole in it had already grown numb, and he could no longer feel his big toe. Besides that, his whole body began to feel colder and colder.

The thought that he might, and very probably would, die that night occurred to him, but did not seem particularly unpleasant or dreadful. It did not seem particularly unpleasant, because his whole life had been not a continual holiday, but on the contrary an unceasing round of toil of which he was beginning to feel weary. And it did not seem particularly dreadful, because besides the masters he had served here, like Vasíli Andréevich, he always felt himself dependent on the Chief Master, who had sent him into this life, and he knew that when dying he would still be in that Master's power and would not be ill-used by Him. 'It seems a pity to give up what one is used to and accustomed to. But there's nothing to be done, I shall get used to the new things.'

'Sins?' he thought, and remembered his drunkenness, the money that had gone on drink, how he had offended his wife, his cursing, his neglect of church and of the fasts, and all the things the priest blamed him for at confession. 'Of course they are sins. But then, did I take them on of myself? That's evidently how God made me. Well, and the sins? Where am I to escape to?'

So at first he thought of what might happen to him that night, and then did not return to such thoughts but gave himself up to whatever recollections came into his head of themselves. Now he thought of Martha's arrival, of the drunkenness among the workers and his own renunciation of drink, then of their present journey and of Tarás's house and the talk about the breaking-up of the family, then of his own lad, and of Mukhórty now sheltered under the drugget, and then of his master who made the sledge creak as he tossed about in it. 'I expect you're sorry yourself that you started out, dear man,' he thought. 'It would seem hard to leave a life such as his! It's not like the likes of us.'

Then all these recollections began to grow confused and got mixed in his head, and he fell asleep.

But when Vasíli Andréevich, getting on the horse, jerked the sledge, against the back of which Nikíta was leaning, and it shifted away and hit him in the back with one of its runners, he awoke and had to change his position whether he liked it or not. Straightening his legs with difficulty and shaking the snow off them he got up, and an agonizing cold immediately penetrated his whole body. On making out what was happening he called to Vasíli Andréevich to leave him the drugget which the horse no longer needed, so that he might wrap himself in it.

But Vasíli Andréevich did not stop, but disappeared amid the powdery snow.

Left alone, Nikíta considered for a moment what he should do. He felt that he had not the strength to go off in search of a house. It was no longer possible to sit down in his old place—it was by now all filled with snow. He felt that he could not get warmer in the sledge either, for there was nothing to cover himself with, and his coat and sheepskin no longer warmed him at all. He felt as cold as though he had nothing on but a shirt. He became frightened. 'Lord, heavenly Father!' he muttered, and was comforted by the consciousness that he was not alone but that there was One who heard him and would not abandon him. He gave a deep sigh, and keeping the sackcloth over his head he got inside the sledge and lay down in the place where his master had been.

But he could not get warm in the sledge either. At first he shivered all over, then the shivering ceased and little by little he began to lose consciousness. He did not know whether he was dying or falling asleep, but felt equally prepared for the one as for the other.

VIII

Meanwhile Vasíli Andréevich, with his feet and the ends of the reins, urged the horse on in the direction in which for some reason he expected the forest and forester's hut to be. The snow covered his eyes and the wind seemed intent on stopping him, but bending forward and constantly lapping his coat over and pushing it between himself and the cold harness pad which prevented him from sitting properly, he kept urging the horse on. Mukhórty ambled on obediently though with difficulty, in the direction in which he was driven.

Vasíli Andréevich rode for about five minutes straight ahead, as he thought, seeing nothing but the horse's head and the white waste, and hearing only the whistle of the wind about the horse's ears and his coat collar.

Suddenly a dark patch showed up in front of him. His heart beat with joy, and he rode towards the object, already seeing in imagination the walls of village houses. But the dark patch was not stationary, it kept moving; and it was not a village but some tall stalks of wormwood sticking up through the snow on the boundary between two fields, and desperately tossing about under the pressure of the wind which beat it all to one side and whistled through it. The sight of that wormwood tormented by the pitiless wind made Vasíli Andréevich shudder, he knew not why, and he hurriedly began urging the horse on, not noticing that when riding up to the wormwood he had quite changed his direction and was now heading the opposite way, though still imagining that he was riding towards where the hut should be. But the horse kept making towards the right, and Vasíli Andréevich kept guiding it to the left.

Again something dark appeared in front of him. Again he rejoiced, convinced that now it was certainly a village. But once more it was the same boundary line overgrown with wormwood, once more the same wormwood desperately tossed by the wind and carrying unreasoning terror to his heart. But its being the same wormwood was not all, for beside it there was a horse's track partly snowed over. Vasíli Andréevich stopped, stooped down and looked carefully. It was a horse-track only partially covered with snow, and could be none but his own horse's hoofprints. He had evidently gone round in a small circle. 'I shall perish like that!' he thought, and not to give way to his terror he urged on the horse still more, peering into the snowy darkness in which he saw only flitting and fitful points of light. Once he thought he heard the barking of dogs or the howling of wolves, but the sounds were so faint and indistinct that he did not know whether he heard them or merely imagined them, and he stopped and began to listen intently.

Suddenly some terrible, deafening cry resounded near his ears, and everything shivered and shook under him. He seized Mukhórty's neck, but that too was shaking all over and the terrible cry grew still more frightful. For some seconds Vasíli Andréevich could not collect himself or understand what was happening. It was only that Mukhórty, whether to encourage himself or to call for help, had neighed loudly and resonantly. 'Ugh, you wretch! How you frightened me, damn you!' thought Vasíli Andréevich. But even when he understood the cause of his terror he could not shake it off.

'I must calm myself and think things over,' he said to himself, but yet he could not stop, and continued to urge the horse on, without noticing that he was now going with the wind instead of against it. His body, especially between his legs where it touched the pad of the harness and was not covered by his overcoats, was getting painfully cold, especially when the horse walked slowly. His legs and arms trembled and his breathing came fast. He saw himself perishing amid this dreadful snowy waste, and could see no means of escape.

Suddenly the horse under him tumbled into something and, sinking into a snow-drift, began to plunge and fell on his side. Vasíli Andréevich jumped off, and in so doing dragged to one side the breechband on which his foot was resting, and twisted round the pad to which he held as he dismounted. As soon as he had jumped off, the horse struggled to his feet, plunged forward, gave one leap and another, neighed again, and dragging the drugget and the breechband after him, disappeared, leaving Vasíli Andréevich alone on the snow-drift.

The latter pressed on after the horse, but the snow lay so deep and his coats were so heavy that, sinking above his knees at each step, he stopped breathless after taking not more than twenty steps. 'The copse, the oxen, the leasehold, the shop, the tavern, the house with the iron-roofed barn, and my heir,' thought he. 'How can I leave all that? What does this mean? It cannot be!' These thoughts flashed through his mind. Then he thought of the wormwood tossed by the wind, which he had twice ridden past, and he was seized with such terror that he did not believe in the reality of what was happening to him. 'Can this be a dream?' he thought, and tried to wake up but could not. It was real snow that lashed his face and covered him and chilled his right hand from which he had lost the glove, and this was a real desert in which he was now left alone like that wormwood, awaiting an inevitable, speedy, and meaningless death.

'Queen of Heaven! Holy Father Nicholas, teacher of temperance!' he thought, recalling the service of the day before and the holy icon with its black face and gilt frame, and the tapers which he sold to be set before that icon and which were almost immediately brought back to him scarcely burnt at all, and which he put away in the store-chest. He began to pray to that same Nicholas the Wonder-Worker to save him, promising him a thanksgiving service and some candles. But he clearly and indubitably realized that the icon, its frame, the candles, the priest, and the thanksgiving service, though very important and necessary in church, could do nothing for him here, and that there was and could be no connexion between those candles and services and his present disastrous plight. 'I must not despair,' he thought. 'I must follow the horse's track before it is snowed under. He will lead me out, or I may even catch him. Only I must not hurry, or I shall stick fast and be more lost than ever.'

But in spite of his resolution to go quietly, he rushed forward and even ran, continually falling, getting up and falling again. The horse's track was already hardly visible in places where the snow did not lie deep. 'I am lost!' thought Vasíli Andréevich. 'I shall lose the track and not catch the horse.' But at that moment he saw something black. It was Mukhórty, and not only Mukhórty, but the sledge with the shafts and the kerchief. Mukhórty, with the sacking and the breechband twisted round to one side, was standing not in his former place but nearer to the shafts, shaking his head which the reins he was stepping on drew downwards. It turned out that Vasíli Andréevich had sunk in the same ravine Nikíta had previously fallen into, and that Mukhórty had been bringing him back to the sledge and he had got off his back no more than fifty paces from where the sledge was.

IX

Having stumbled back to the sledge Vasíli Andréevich caught hold of it and for a long time stood motionless, trying to calm himself and recover his breath. Nikíta was not in his former place, but something, already covered with snow, was lying in the sledge and Vasíli Andréevich concluded that this was Nikíta. His terror had now quite left him, and if he felt any fear it was lest the dreadful terror should return that he had experienced when on the horse and especially when he was left alone in the snowdrift. At any cost he had to avoid that terror, and to keep it away he must do something—occupy himself with something. And the first thing he did was to turn his back to the wind and open his fur coat. Then, as soon as he recovered his breath a little, he shook the snow out of his boots and out of his left-hand glove (the right-hand glove was hopelessly lost and by this time probably lying somewhere under a dozen inches of snow); then as was his custom when going out of his shop to buy grain from the peasants, he pulled his girdle low down and tightened it and prepared for action. The first thing that occurred to him was to free Mukhórty's leg from the rein. Having done that, and tethered him to the iron cramp at the front of the sledge where he had been before, he was going round the horse's quarters to put the breechband and pad straight and cover him with the cloth, but at that moment he noticed that something was moving in the sledge and Nikíta's head rose up out of the snow that covered it. Nikíta, who was half frozen, rose with great difficulty and sat up, moving his hand before his nose in a strange manner just as if he were driving away flies. He waved his hand and said something, and seemed to Vasíli Andréevich to be calling him. Vasíli Andréevich left the cloth unadjusted and went up to the sledge.

'What is it?' he asked. 'What are you saying?'

'I'm dy . . . ing, that's what,' said Nikíta brokenly and with difficulty. 'Give what is owing to me to my lad, or to my wife, no matter.'

'Why, are you really frozen?' asked Vasíli Andréevich.

'I feel it's my death. Forgive me for Christ's sake . . .' said Nikíta in a tearful voice, continuing to wave his hand before his face as if driving away flies.

Vasíli Andréevich stood silent and motionless for half a minute. Then suddenly, with the same resolution with which he used to strike hands when making a good purchase, he took a step back and turning up his sleeves began raking the snow off Nikíta and out of the sledge. Having done this he hurriedly undid his girdle, opened out his fur coat, and having pushed Nikíta down, lay down on top of him, covering him not only with his fur coat but with the whole of his body, which glowed with warmth. After pushing the skirts of his coat between Nikíta and the sides of the sledge, and holding down its hem with his knees, Vasíli Andréevich lay like that face down, with his head pressed against the front of the sledge. Here he no longer heard the horse's movements or the whistling of the wind, but only Nikíta's breathing. At first and for a long time Nikíta lay motionless, then he sighed deeply and moved.

'There, and you say you are dying! Lie still and get warm, that's our way . . .' began Vasíli Andréevich.

But to his great surprise he could say no more, for tears came to his eyes and his lower jaw began to quiver rapidly. He stopped speaking and only gulped down the risings in his throat. 'Seems I was badly frightened and have gone quite weak,' he thought. But this weakness was not only not unpleasant, but gave him a peculiar joy such as he had never felt before.

'That's our way!' he said to himself, experiencing a strange and solemn tenderness. He lay like that for a long time, wiping his eyes on the fur of his coat and tucking under his knee the right skirt, which the wind kept turning up.

But he longed so passionately to tell somebody of his joyful condition that he said: 'Nikíta!'

'It's comfortable, warm!' came a voice from beneath.

'There, you see, friend, I was going to perish. And you would have been frozen, and I should have . . .'

But again his jaws began to quiver and his eyes to fill with tears, and he could say no more.

'Well, never mind,' he thought. 'I know about myself what I know.'

He remained silent and lay like that for a long time.

Nikíta kept him warm from below and his fur coats from above. Only his hands, with which he kept his coat-skirts down round Nikíta's sides, and his legs which the wind kept uncovering, began to freeze, especially his right hand which had no glove. But he did not think of his legs or of his hands but only of how to warm the peasant who was lying under him. He looked out several times at Mukhórty and could see that his back was uncovered and the drugget and breeching lying on the snow, and that he ought to get up and cover him, but he could not bring himself to leave Nikíta and disturb even for a moment the joyous condition he was in. He no longer felt any kind of terror.

'No fear, we shan't lose him this time!' he said to himself, referring to his getting the peasant warm with the same boastfulness with which he spoke of his buying and selling.

Vasíli Andréevich lay in that way for one hour, another, and a third, but he was unconscious of the passage of time. At first impressions of the snow-storm, the sledge-shafts, and the horse with the shaft-bow shaking before his eyes, kept passing through his mind, then he remembered Nikíta lying under him, then recollections of the festival, his wife, the police-officer, and the box of candles, began to mingle with these; then again Nikíta, this time lying under that box, then the peasants, customers and traders, and the white walls of his house with its iron roof with Nikíta lying underneath, presented themselves to his imagination. Afterwards all these impressions blended into one nothingness. As the colours of the rainbow unite into one white light, so all these different impressions mingled into one, and he fell asleep.

For a long time he slept without dreaming, but just before dawn the visions recommenced. It seemed to him that he was standing by the box of tapers and that Tíkhon's wife was asking for a five-kopek taper for the Church fête. He wished to take one out and give it to her, but his hands would not lift, being held tight in his pockets. He wanted to walk round the box but his feet would not move and his new clean goloshes had grown to the stone floor, and he could neither lift them nor get his feet out of the goloshes. Then the taper-box was no longer a box but a bed, and suddenly Vasíli Andréevich saw himself lying in his bed at home. He was lying in his bed and could not get up. Yet it was necessary for him to get up because Iván Matvéich, the police-officer, would soon call for him and he had to go with him—either to bargain for the forest or to put Mukhórty's breeching straight

He asked his wife: 'Nikoláevna, hasn't be come yet?' 'No, he hasn't,' she replied. He heard someone drive up to the front steps. 'It must be him.' 'No, he's gone past.' 'Nikoláevna! I say, Nikoláevna, isn't he here yet?' 'No.' He was still lying on his bed and could not get up, but was always waiting. And this waiting was uncanny and yet joyful. Then suddenly his joy was completed. He whom he was expecting came; not Iván Matvéich the police-officer, but someone else—yet it was he whom he had been waiting for. He came and called him; and it was he who had called him and told him to lie down on Nikíta. And Vasíli Andréevich was glad that that one had come for him.

'I'm coming!' he cried joyfully, and that cry awoke him, but woke him up not at all the same person he had been when he fell asleep. He tried to get up but could not, tried to move his arm and could not, to move his leg and also could not, to turn his head and could not. He was surprised but not at all disturbed by this. He understood that this was death, and was not at all disturbed by that either. He remembered that Nikíta was lying under him and that he had got warm and was alive, and it seemed to him that he was Nikíta and Nikíta was he, and that his life was not in himself but in Nikíta. He strained his ears and heard Nikíta breathing and even slightly snoring. 'Nikíta is alive, so I too am alive!' he said to himself triumphantly.

And he remembered his money, his shop, his house, the buying and selling, and Mirónov's millions, and it was hard for him to understand why that man, called Vasíli Brekhunóv, had troubled himself with all those things with which he had been troubled.

'Well, it was because he did not know what the real thing was,' he thought, concerning that Vasíli Brekhunóv. 'He did not know, but now I know and know for sure. Now I know!' And again he heard the voice of the one who had called him before. 'I'm coming! Coming!' he responded gladly, and his whole being was filled with joyful emotion. He felt himself free and that nothing could hold him back any longer.

After that Vasíli Andréevich neither saw, heard, nor felt anything more in this world.

All around the snow still eddied. The same whirlwinds of snow circled about, covering the dead Vasíli Andréevich's fur coat, the shivering Mukhórty, the sledge, now scarcely to be seen, and Nikíta lying at the bottom of it, kept warm beneath his dead master.

X

Nikíta awoke before daybreak. He was aroused by the cold that had begun to creep down his back. He had dreamt that he was coming from the mill with a load of his master's flour and when crossing the stream had missed the bridge and let the cart get stuck. And he saw that he had crawled under the cart and was trying to lift it by arching his back. But strange to say the cart did not move, it stuck to his back and he could neither lift it nor get out from under it. It was crushing the whole of his loins. And how cold it felt! Evidently he must crawl out. 'Have done!' he exclaimed to whoever was pressing the cart down on him. 'Take out the sacks!' But the cart pressed down colder and colder, and then he heard a strange knocking, awoke completely, and remembered everything. The cold cart was his dead and frozen master lying upon him. And the knock was produced by Mukhórty, who had twice struck the sledge with his hoof.

'Andréevich! Eh, Andréevich!' Nikíta called cautiously, beginning to realize the truth, and straightening his back. But Vasíli Andréevich did not answer and his stomach and legs were stiff and cold and heavy like iron weights.

'He must have died! May the Kingdom of Heaven be his!' thought Nikíta.

He turned his head, dug with his hand through the snow about him and opened his eyes. It was daylight; the wind was whistling as before between the shafts, and the snow was falling in the same way, except that it was no longer driving against the frame of the sledge but silently covered both sledge and horse deeper and deeper, and neither the horse's movements nor his breathing were any longer to be heard.

'He must have frozen too,' thought Nikíta of Mukhórty, and indeed those hoof knocks against the sledge, which had awakened Nikíta, were the last efforts the already numbed Mukhórty had made to keep on his feet before dying.

'O Lord God, it seems Thou art calling me too!' said Nikíta. 'Thy Holy Will be done. But it's uncanny. . . . Still, a man can't die twice and must die once. If only it would come soon!'

And he again drew in his head, closed his eyes, and became unconscious, fully convinced that now he was certainly and finally dying.

It was not till noon that day that peasants dug Vasíli Andréevich and Nikíta out of the snow with their shovels, not more than seventy yards from the road and less than half a mile from the village.

The snow had hidden the sledge, but the shafts and the kerchief tied to them were still visible. Mukhórty, buried up to his belly in snow, with the breeching and drugget hanging down, stood all white, his dead head pressed against his frozen throat: icicles hung from his nostrils, his eyes were covered with hoar-frost as though filled with tears, and he had grown so thin in that one night that he was nothing but skin and bone.

Vasíli Andréevich was stiff as a frozen carcass, and when they rolled him off Nikíta his legs remained apart and his arms stretched out as they had been. His bulging hawk eyes were frozen, and his open mouth under his clipped moustache was full of snow. But Nikíta though chilled through was still alive. When he had been brought to, he felt sure that he was already dead and that what was taking place with him was no longer happening in this world but in the next. When he heard the peasants shouting as they dug him out and rolled the frozen body of Vasíli Andréevich from off him, he was at first surprised that in the other world peasants should be shouting in the same old way and had the same kind of body, and then when he realized that he was still in this world he was sorry rather than glad, especially when he found that the toes on both his feet were frozen.

Nikíta lay in hospital for two months. They cut off three of his toes, but the others recovered so that he was still able to work and went on living for another twenty years, first as a farm-labourer, then in his old age as a watchman. He died at home as he had wished, only this year, under the icons with a lighted taper in his hands. Before he died he asked his wife's forgiveness and forgave her for the cooper. He also took leave of his son and grandchildren, and died sincerely glad that he was relieving his son and daughter-in-law of the burden of having to feed him, and that he was now really passing from this life of which he was weary into that other life which every year and every hour grew clearer and more desirable to him. Whether he is better or worse off there where he awoke after his death, whether he was disappointed or found there what he expected, we shall all soon learn.

ALYOSHA THE POT

[1905]

•

Alyosha was a younger brother. He was nicknamed "the Pot", because once, when his mother sent him with a pot of milk for the deacon's wife, he stumbled and broke it. His mother thrashed him soundly, and the children in the village began to tease him, calling him "the Pot". Alyosha the Pot: and this is how he got his nickname.

Alyosha was a skinny little fellow, lop-eared—his ears stuck out like wings—and with a large nose. The children always teased him about this, too, saying, "Alyosha has a nose like a gourd on a pole!"

There was a school in the village where Alyosha lived, but reading and writing and such did not come easy for him, and besides there was no time to learn. His older brother lived with a merchant in town, and Alyosha had begun helping his father when still a child. When he was only six years old, he was already watching over his family's cow and sheep with his younger sister in the common pasture. And long before he was grown, he had started taking care of their horses day and night. From his twelfth year he plowed and carted. He hardly had the strength for all these chores, but he did have a certain manner—he was always cheerful. When the children laughed at him, he fell silent or laughed himself. If his father cursed him, he stood quietly and listened. And when they finished and ignored him again, he smiled and went back to whatever task was before him.

When Alyosha was nineteen years old, his brother was taken into the army; and his father arranged for Alyosha to take his brother's place as a servant in the merchant's household. He was given his brother's old boots and his father's cap and coat and was taken into town. Alyosha was very pleased with his new clothes, but the merchant was quite dissatisfied with his appearance.

"I thought you would bring me a young man just like Semyon," said the merchant, looking Alyosha over carefully. "But you've brought me such a sniveller. What's he good for?"

"Ah, he can do anything—harness and drive anywhere you like. And he's a glutton for work. Only looks like a stick. He's really very wiry."

"That much is plain. Well, we shall see."

"And above all he's a meek one. Loves to work."

"Well, what can I do? Leave him."

And so Alyosha began to live with the merchant.

The merchant's family was not large. There were his wife, his old mother and three children. His older married son, who had only completed grammar school, was in business with his father. His other son, a studious sort, had been graduated from the high school and was for a time at the university, though he had been expelled and now lived at home. And there was a daughter, too, a young girl in the high school.

At first they did not like Alyosha. He was too much the peasant and was poorly dressed. He had no manners and addressed everyone familiarly as in the country. But soon they grew used to him. He was a better servant than his brother and was always very responsive. Whatever they set him to do he did willingly and quickly, moving from one task to another without stopping. And at the merchant's, just as at home, all the work was given to Alyosha. The more he did, the more everyone heaped upon him. The mistress of the household and her old mother-in-law, and the daughter, and the younger son, even the merchant's clerk and the cook—all sent him here and sent him there and ordered him to do everything that they could think of. The only thing that Alyosha ever heard was "Run do this, fellow", or "Alyosha, fix this up now", or "Did you forget, Alyosha? Look here, fellow, don't you forget!" And Alyosha ran, and fixed, and looked, and did not forget, and managed to do everything and smiled all the while.

Alyosha soon wore out his brother's boots, and the merchant scolded him sharply for walking about in tatters with his bare feet sticking out and ordered him to buy new boots in the market. These boots were truly new, and Alyosha was very happy with them; but his feet remained old all the same, and by evening they ached so from running that he got mad at them. Alyosha was afraid that when his father came to collect his wages, he would be very annoyed that the master had deducted the cost of the new boots from his pay.

In winter Alyosha got up before dawn, chopped firewood, swept out the courtyard, fed grain to the cow and the horses and watered them. Afterwards, he lit the stoves, cleaned the boots and coats of all the household, got out the samovars and polished them. Then, either the clerk called him into the shop to take out the wares or the cook ordered him to knead the dough and to wash the pans. And later he would be sent into town with a message, or to the school for the daughter, or to fetch lamp oil or something else for the master's old mother. "Where have you been loafing, you worthless thing?" one would say to him, and then another. Or among themselves they would say, "Why go yourself? Alyosha will run for you. Alyosha, Alyosha!" And Alyosha would run.

Alyosha always ate breakfast on the run and was seldom in time for dinner. The cook was always chiding him, because he never took meals with the others, but for all that she did feel sorry for him and always left him something hot for dinner and for supper.

Before and during holidays there was a lot more work for Alyosha, though he was happier during holidays, because then everyone gave him tips, not much, only about sixty kopeks usually; but it was his own money, which he could spend as he chose. He never laid eyes on his wages, for his father always came into town and took from the merchant Alyosha's pay, giving him only the rough edge of his tongue for wearing out his brother's boots too quickly. When he had saved two rubles altogether from tips, Alyosha bought on the cook's advice a red knitted sweater. When he put it on for the first time and looked down at himself, he was so surprised and delighted that he just stood in the kitchen gaping and gulping.

Alyosha said very little, and when he did speak, it was always to say something necessary abruptly and briefly. And when he was told to do something or other or was asked if he could do it, he always answered without the slightest hesitation "I can do it". And he would immediately throw himself into the job and do it.

Alyosha did not know how to pray at all. His mother had once taught him the words, but he had forgot even as she spoke. Nonetheless, he did pray, morning and evening, but simply, just with his hands, crossing himself.

Thus Alyosha lived for a year and a half, and then, during the second half of the second year, the most unusual experience of his life occurred. This experience was his sudden discovery, to his complete amazement, that besides those relationships between people that arise from the need that one may have for another, there also exist other relationships that are completely different: not a relationship that a person has with another because that other is needed to clean boots, to run errands or to harness horses; but a relationship that a person has with another who is in no way necessary to him, simply because that other one wants to serve him and to be loving to him. And he discovered, too, that he, Alyosha, was just such a person. He realized all this through the cook Ustinja. Ustinja was an orphan, a young girl yet, and as hard a worker as Alyosha. She began to feel sorry for Alyosha, and Alyosha for the first time in his life felt that he himself, not his services, but he himself was needed by another person. When his mother had been kind to him or had felt sorry for him, he took no notice of it, because it seemed to him so natural a thing, just the same as if he felt sorry for himself. But suddenly he realized that Ustinja, though completely a stranger, felt sorry for him, too. She always left him a pot of kasha with butter, and when he ate, she sat with him, watching him with her chin propped upon her fist. And when he looked up at her and she smiled, he, too, smiled.

It was all so new and so strange that at first Alyosha was frightened. He felt that it disturbed his work, his serving, but he was nonetheless very happy. And when he happened to look down and notice his trousers, which Ustinja had mended for him, he would shake his head and smile. Often while he was working or running an errand, he would think of Ustinja and mutter warmly "Ah, that Ustinja!" Ustinja helped him as best she could, and he helped her. She told him all about her life, how she had been orphaned when very young, how an old aunt had taken her in, how this aunt later sent her into town to work, how the merchant's son had tried stupidly to seduce her, and how she put him in his place. She loved to talk, and he found listening to her very pleasant. Among other things he heard that in town it often happened that peasant boys who came to serve in households would marry the cooks. And once she asked him if his parents would marry him off soon. He replied that he didn't know and that there was no one in his village whom he wanted.

"What, then, have you picked out someone else?" she asked.

"Yes. I'd take you. Will you?"

"O Pot, my Pot, how cunningly you put it to me!" she said, cuffing him playfully on the back with her ladle.

At Shrovetide Alyosha's old father came into town again to collect his son's wages. The merchant's wife had found out that Alyosha planned to marry Ustinja, and she was not at all pleased. "She will just get pregnant, and then what good will she be!" she complained to her husband.

The merchant counted out Alyosha's money to his father. "Well, is my boy doing all right by you?" asked the old man. "I told you he was a meek one, would do anything you say."

"Meek or no, he's done something stupid. He has got it into his head to marry the cook. And I will not keep married servants. It doesn't suit us."

"Eh, that little fool! What a fool! How can he think to do such a stupid thing! But don't worry over it. I'll make him forget all that nonsense."

The old man walked straight into the kitchen and sat down at the table to wait for his son. Alyosha was, as always, running an errand, but he soon came in all out of breath.

"Well, I thought you were a sensible fellow, but what nonsense you've thought up!" Aloysha's father greeted him.

"I've done nothing."

"What d'you mean nothing! You've decided to marry. I'll marry you when the time comes, and I'll marry you to whoever I want, not to some town slut."

The old man said a great deal more of the same sort. Alyosha stood quietly and sighed. When his father finished, he smiled.

"So I'll forget about it," he said.

"See that you do right now," the old man said curtly as he left.

When his father had gone and Alyosha remained alone with Ustinja, who had been standing behind the kitchen door listening while his father was talking, he said to her: "Our plan won't work out. Did you hear? He was furious, won't let us."

Ustinja began to cry quietly into her apron. Alyosha clucked his tongue and said, "How could I not obey him? Look, we must forget all about it."

In the evening, when the merchant's wife called him to close the shutters, she said to him, "Are you going to obey your father and forget all this nonsense about marrying?"

"Yes. Of course. I've forgot it," Alyosha said quickly, then smiled and immediately began weeping.

From that time Alyosha did not speak again to Ustinja about marriage and lived as he had before.

One morning during Lent the clerk sent Alyosha to clear the snow off the roof. He crawled up onto the roof, shovelled it clean and began to break up the frozen snow near the gutters when his feet slipped out from under him and he fell headlong with his shovel. As ill luck would have it, he fell not into the snow, but onto an entry-way with an iron railing. Ustinja ran up to him, followed by the merchant's daughter.

"Are you hurt, Alyosha?"

"Yes. But it's nothing. Nothing."

He wanted to get up, but he could not and just smiled. Others came and carried him down into the yard-keeper's lodge. An orderly from the hospital arrived, examined him and asked where he hurt. "It hurts all over," he replied. "But it's nothing. Nothing. Only the master will be annoyed. Must send word to Papa."

Alyosha lay abed for two full days, and then, on the third day, they sent for a priest.

"You're not going to die, are you?" asked Ustinja.

"Well, we don't all live forever. It must be some time," he answered quickly, as always. 'Thank you, dear Ustinja, for feeling sorry for me. See, it's better they didn't let us marry, for nothing would have come of it. And now all is fine."

He prayed with the priest, but only with his hands and with his heart. And in his heart he felt that if he was good here, if he obeyed and did not offend, then there all would be well.

He said little. He only asked for something to drink and smiled wonderingly. Then he seemed surprised at something, and stretched out and died.

AN EXTRA STORY

LIFE EXPECTANCY

FROM *GIRL TROUBLE*
BY HOLLY GODDARD JONES

AVAILABLE FROM HARPER PERENNIAL
IN SEPTEMBER 2009

Coach Theo Burke was standing outside his classroom during morning break when he noticed Josie across the hall, pinned up against a locker. One of the varsity basketball players, Jatarius, was doing the pinning—his near-seven feet making Josie seem almost short in comparison, big hands straddling her shoulders, too-handsome black face leaned in to kissing distance. The worst thing—the thing that felt like a punch in the gut—was the look on Josie's face, a look Theo knew well. Her head was tilted, and she was smiling, but just a little: that smart smile, that sexy half-smile with the bottom lip barely caught under her front teeth, an expression that Theo recognized as the smallest bit calculated but mostly genuine. Mostly the only way Josie knew how to be.

He strode over, hands shoved so deep in his khakis that his watch got caught on one side. He cleared his throat.

"Jatarius," Theo said.

"Yeah." A slow breath, dusky, directed on Josie and not at him. "Move it along."

Jatarius pulled to a slow stand, languid, his skin gleaming as if oiled. "Just talking, Coach," he said, and Josie giggled. Theo turned to her, and she looked away.

"You're supposed to be swapping books now, not talking," he said, realizing as he said it how ridiculous—how *old*—he sounded. Josie was losing interest in him, and all he had to cling to was his authority as her teacher and her coach. Her better. And how false that felt, watching her, knowing what her breasts looked like beneath that t-shirt and hooded sweatshirt: small, spread apart—a tall girl's breasts.

Jatarius pulled his bookbag up over his shoulder. "See ya," he told Josie, and she fluttered her fingers at him as he sauntered off.

"What are you doing?" Theo whispered, looking around to make sure nobody was watching them.

She tried to laugh again, but her voice caught a little, and she stopped. Her eyes were over-bright, her shoulders stiff, but she smiled—for him, for the group of girls crossing behind him. "I'm pregnant, Coach," she said. She opened her mouth, then closed it again. She shrugged.

The bell rang, and Theo turned to walk back into his classroom, where twenty-six sophomores were waiting to learn about the Fertile Crescent, the first bloom of civilization.

Abortion, she told him. Soon, now, so I don't have to miss any game time. Right away. Yesterday.

"All right," Theo said, fanning the air with his palms, a gesture implying *calm down* that he used when students freaked out about a bad test score or got into fights. He and Josie were in his coach's office. He'd let practice out early that day, after only an hour. Josie had seemed normal—made her warm-up sprints at top speed, missed only a single basket as they ran figure-eights—but *he* could barely concentrate enough to follow the action or to guide the girls to the next drill. They looked the same out there in their practice jerseys and white high-tops: lanky girls with brown ponytails and acne. Only Josie stood out, her gold hair alight under the gym's fluorescents. Only Josie seemed real. "All right, slow down. Give me a minute."

She looked at her hands, as if she were counting off the seconds. "Antibiotics," she said finally. "I was sick over Christmas break. That's what did it."

Theo was thinking: *baby*. He had a baby, and a wife. His baby was eleven months old, and they called her Sissy, short for Cecily. Five months ago they found out that her breathing problems were caused by cystic fibrosis, which turned the name—their affection—into a lousy pun, a cruel joke. "Wait," he said. "What? Did what?"

"The antibiotics affected the Pill," she said. "I looked it up on the Internet. At least I'll know better from now on."

"From now on?"

"Jesus," she said. "I'm eighteen. I'm not going to stop having sex."

"I'm just saying," Theo said. He wondered, despite himself, if she would still want to have sex with him.

She pulled a package of gum out her purse and unwrapped a piece. "I'm just ready to get this over with," she said, now chewing. "I've got a lot to worry about. School and all."

"Of course," Theo said. She was going to Western Kentucky University in the fall, a full ride. He had helped her get it. He had posed with her, her mother, and Western's basketball coach three months ago when they signed the letter of intent, and the photo ran in the *News Leader*. "Cute girl," his wife had said when she saw it. And Theo—who was already meeting Josie for fast screws in his office and his car and a few times at her house, when her mother was pulling seconds at the sewing factory—had only nodded.

Now Josie sat in the chair opposite Theo's, the desk between them, and played with the end of her thick, yellow braid, wanting, he saw, to put it into her mouth. He'd done his best to tease her out of that habit, seeing it as the one solid piece of evidence between them—other than the obvious facts of their positions as teacher and student, of course—that being together was scuzzy and wrong, an embarrassment to them both. Because in so many other ways, it hardly seemed like a problem at all. She'd turned eighteen in December, and she was about to graduate. She was mature. She had a good future ahead of her. There was the infidelity, but Theo tried, with some success, to keep his home life and school life separate, and it seemed to him that he was okay—getting by, at least—as long as he was able to do what had to be done in both lives. He was an average teacher, but better than most coaches: he liked his World Civ classes and tolerated Kentucky Studies. At least he wasn't just popping a movie in the VCR every day, like Mathias, the boys' basketball coach, who famously screened *Quigley Down Under* for his freshman geography students during their Australia unit. He thought that he was a better than average father, at least most of the time. He'd hoped for a son, sure—pictured a boy all those years he and Mia were trying and failing to conceive, a boy to play basketball with and to fish with, all of the clichés. But he'd been happy with his girl, and if her delicacy dismayed him a little—how could it not?—in so many ways, it only made him love her more.

Some days, driving home from work, he thought, *I have a house*, and was instantly filled with pride. House, yes—he was a man, all right. *I have a wife. I have a child.* Before coming in the front door, he could picture all three, house, wife, daughter, as they ought to be: clean, happy, healthy. *This is my life*, he'd think, and then he'd open the door.

"My mom probably wouldn't be too upset if she knew," Josie said. "She likes you. She doesn't get hung up on stuff like you being a teacher. She'd take care of it if she had the money to, but she doesn't."

"How much?" Theo asked.

Josie shook her head. "I don't know yet."

How much was an abortion? Two hundred dollars? A thousand? He tried to imagine withdrawing that much money from the checking account without Mia noticing. Mia was in her own world a lot of the time these days, but she could surprise him with her sudden sharpness.

"But you'll take care of this, right?" Josie said. She was going to cry, he was sure. *Put the braid in your mouth*, he thought. *Do it if that'll shut you up.* "Right?" Josie said.

No less than five hundred, he bet. But he could scrounge it up. Mathias might loan it to him out of his pot fund. Theo could pay it back slowly that way, twenty this week, fifty the next. There wasn't any question, though; it had to be done. His job paid for shit—and he'd have to pick up something part-time this summer, probably, just to make ends meet—but it was all he had, and the insurance was good. He couldn't lose that. Not with Sissy to worry about.

"Okay," Theo told her. "You get the information and set it up, and I'll pay for it."

"And drive me," Josie said. "I can't ask Mama to do that."

"Okay, I'll drive you," Theo said.

She pulled the rubber band off the end of her braid and raked her fingers through the thick weave of her hair, setting it loose. It ran over her shoulders, halfway down her back, wavy and almost iridescent. Rapunzel hair, he'd always thought. Her nose and cheeks were freckled, and she had that balance between strength and delicacy that most of his girl athletes lacked. Miraculous.

"We could have sex," she said, almost with resignation.

He nodded.

When Sissy's cystic fibrosis was confirmed, the doctors threw a lot of numbers at Theo and Mia, too many to make sense of. Life expectancy. Percentage of cases in the U.S. Chances of this, chances of that. But the fact that stayed with Theo— the data that confirmed for him everything wrong with his marriage and his life—was this: a child could only get the disease if both parents carried a defective gene. Defective, the doctor's word. Dr. Travis—the first of several—told them this in his wood-paneled office with the dark green carpeting, and Theo could remember thinking he, Mia, and Sissy, who was too small at six months but still porcelain-pretty, were now lost in the woods together. He and Mia, two unknowing defectives, had somehow found each other, beaten the odds, and brought forth a child who was drowning in her own chest because the two of them should never have been together in the first place.

When he came home that night after making arrangements with Josie, Mia was in the old recliner, Sissy in her lap, and they were rocking, watching TV. Mia's bare foot bobbed above the floor, keeping time. The house was filthy, and Theo was nauseous at the smells that assaulted him as soon as he walked in the door: soured food stuck to the dishes that were piled up on the kitchen countertops; the heavy metallic tang of piss, where the toilet hadn't been flushed; and shit, too, he was sure of it. Maybe the baby's, but probably the dog's. Mia took care of Sissy to the point of obsession, but she seemed to forget that they had a dog—a Beagle mix they'd gotten free from an unplanned litter—though bringing him home was her idea. She'd read in some magazine that dog owners had longer life expectancies, and cancer patients with dogs more often went into remission or had spontaneous recoveries. He didn't ask her how the cancer thing was supposed to apply to their daughter.

"Smells like crap in here," Theo told her, setting his briefcase and duffel bag down by the front door.

"I hadn't noticed," Mia said. "Baby-Girl's clean." As if in support, Sissy erupted into one of her chants: *ma ma ma ma ma MAAAA!* Theo picked Sissy up and kissed her clean neck, trying to fill his nose with her scent. She hooked her small hand and paper-thin fingernails into his ear and twisted. "Ma," she said again.

"I hear you," Theo told her. She hasn't said it once.

"Might be the dog," Mia said. She kept watching TV, and Theo knew what she was thinking just as clearly as if she'd spoken out loud: *You'll take care of this, right?*

Theo put Sissy down, his stomach already starting to churn. "I'd say that's the most likely option." He whistled and walked around, trying to find the source of the smell. "Joe!" he yelled, whistling again. The odor, thick, sickly, seemed to be everywhere at first; then he rounded a corner, and it hit him like an arrow, coming from the bedroom. He got down on his knees and looked under the bed.

"Christ," he said. "Fuck."

Joe was in the corner, far from the bed as he could get, and Theo could see the fast rise and fall of the dog's stomach. "Hey, boy." The dog cowered at first—his eyes, so eerily human, rolled up at him warily—then let Theo lift him and carry him into the living room like a baby.

"Dog's sick," Theo told Mia.

She nodded.

"Did he get into something?"

"I don't know. He was out back for a few hours. Maybe he got into the garbage." She was still watching the TV. "Poor boy," she said without interest. "Should we take him to the vet?"

"Probably just needs to finish his business," Theo said, and he went out back to put the dog out. In the low light, he could see Joe make a slow circle in the backyard, then lie down. Theo went back inside and tried his best to clean up the mess, using every chemical he could find under the kitchen sink, moving the bed and pulling up the corner of the carpet so he could get to the pad and sub-floor, too. The smell lingered, and he opened a window.

In the living room, Mia hadn't moved. He sat on the couch and watched what she was watching: a cooking show. Not a regular show, though, like his own mom had watched on PBS when he was in high school—*The Frugal Gourmet* or that one with the old Cajun guy, Justin Wilson—shows where somebody stood behind a counter and cooked the food regular-style. This show had a fattish woman with brown hair, and she looked to be in her own house, because the sunlight seemed real and not put on. The camera zoomed in as she dropped an egg into a mixing bowl, which you didn't see happen on Justin Wilson.

"What is this?" he asked her.

"My favorite show," Mia said. Her voice was dreamy. "This woman owns a restaurant in New England. She cooks very simple foods. She doesn't use margarine, only butter."

"Margarine's better for you," Theo said.

"Not true," Mia told him. They watched as the woman dipped a fancy silver measuring cup into a bowl of sugar. "*This dish is fragrant and delicious*," the woman was saying. "Margarine is a trans fat," Mia continued, "which doesn't break down in your system. Natural foods are better."

"Why do you like this so much?" Theo asked. The woman was now grating lemon peel.

Mia stroked Sissy's arm as she talked. "Her hands. She has such clean hands and fingernails. And her sugar, it doesn't just look like sugar."

Her medication. She'd been a mess since Sissy's birth—post-partum depression, her doctor had said—and she had just started to come back, to be herself again, when Sissy was diagnosed. Her meds were a square dance at this point: Prozac helped for a while, then made her worse than ever. Paxil worked, but they couldn't get the dosage regulated, and the doctor warned them that taking her off it early would result in a major crash. They'd gone on a date a few weeks ago—left Sissy with Mia's mother, tried to dress up and make a night of it—and at the movie, *Million Dollar Baby*, Mia had stared, emotionless, through all the parts that would have had her sobbing a few years before. Theo had asked her what she thought of the story on their drive home, and she seemed confused by her own answer—or not even confused, exactly. Perplexed. Like the changes in her were a cause for a scientific kind of curiosity and nothing else. *I don't know what I thought of it*, she'd said. *I could see that it was sad, but I didn't feel sad. It was intellectual. Is this what being a man is like?*

"Looks like sugar to me," Theo said now.

"Figures."

"You could try making that," Theo told her. "Doesn't look hard. I bet it's real good."

Mia kept rocking. "No, I couldn't do it," she said.

Theo left her and went to the kitchen, unbuttoning his shirt cuffs and rolling up the sleeves to his elbow. He started organizing the dishes and cleaning the counters, pitching empty Lean Cuisine boxes and a Tropicana carton and Ramen noodle bags into a Hefty sack. He couldn't get Josie out of his head, not even for a second. Too easy to think of her, to feel her warm hips between his hands even as he plunged them down into scalding dishwater. He pictured her in the hallway that morning, with Jatarius, and tried to remember the exact look on her face. *You'll take care of this, right?*

He noticed the wet circle in the driveway as he was taking out the trash, but the detail didn't click into place until he was closing the lid of the garbage can, and he realized that Joe wasn't there to meet him. It occurred to him that there wasn't any strewn garbage out back, no sign of disturbance at all, and he remembered the wet spot then—not oil, not water, but anti-freeze, probably leaked out while his car was warming up that morning. He peered into the dark shadows of the far corner of the yard, where the security light didn't hit. "Joe," he said. "Joe, old boy."

There was a tire propped up against the toolshed—Theo had been meaning to take it to the rubber yard behind Kip's Garage for months now—and he found Joe curled up in the space between it and the concrete wall, the thin scrim of green foam on his jowls barely visible in a sliver of moonlight. "Joe," Theo said. He looked at the still body. "Joe," he said again.

The first time he kissed Josie was in August, two weeks before Sissy's diagnosis. Someday, he might be able to blame the whole affair on his difficult home life, on the fear of losing his baby girl before she could have a home and family of her own. Someday, he might be able to forget that those two weeks existed.

When it happened, though, he wasn't thinking of Sissy, or of Mia. He'd known Josie for four years by then, pulling her from JV when she was still in eighth grade—she was that talented— and letting her start power forward on her first game as a high school student. He had recognized in her the quality that would later attract him: the blend of rawness and refinement, power and grace. In the beginning, though, she'd only seemed a grand kind of experiment. What could he turn her into?

The girls came in for mandatory weightlifting in the summer and through September, before real practice started, and the kiss came after one of these late-afternoon sessions. She was telling him about her father—how he left her mother in June to move to Nashville with his new girlfriend, a thirty-year-old wannabe country singer. How her mother had been struggling since then to make ends meet. She wasn't crying, but Theo could tell she wanted to, and the desire he felt for her—until this moment hypothetical and even harmless, like a childhood crush—was overwhelming. So he kissed her. He did it because she looked like she needed it. He did it because he knew he could get away with it.

Now, two days after the dog's death, Theo was determined to make it through a full practice without stopping early or fading out mid-speech, which had been his habit since Josie dropped her news. Some of the girls were beginning to look at him strangely, though he actually wondered more about the ones who weren't. He wondered if Josie had told a friend about the two of them, and if that friend had told a friend. She had always promised him complete secrecy, but he'd worked with young girls long enough to understand how unlikely that was, especially among team-mates. Before the news of her pregnancy, he and Josie had fallen into a strange sort of complacency with one another, an ease that he was now terrified to remember. How careless they had been—with the sex, of course, but also with too-long looks, knowing smiles, risky, ridiculous moments between classes when they passed in the hall and let their fingers brush. They should have been caught already, he knew. They would get caught.

On the court, the girls were running a pass drill. Josie caught the ball, made it around Lisa in three easy strides, and pistoned upward, sinking a two-pointer. She landed hard, and Theo felt his heart wallop. "Josie?" he said.

Her expression was bewildered. "What?"

"Are you okay?"

"Yes," she said testily, already dribbling again.

He'd buried Joe in the backyard, not far from the spot where he died. Mia cried, which was more emotion than Theo could remember seeing from her in a while. He'd dug the grave; then, still sweaty and dirt-streaked, he'd hosed the greasy patch in the driveway, watching the liquid blur, blend, then run off into the grass, indistinguishable from a light rain. *I couldn't have known he'd gotten into that*, Mia had said, and Theo had stripped off his old University of Kentucky sweatshirt and bluejeans without a word, wadding them into a ball and throwing them in the hamper. His muscles, once long and powerful, ached now. *Sissy was coughing again, and I had my hands full. You know how it is.* He'd nodded and started the shower running. *It was your car, for fuck's sake.*

The girls thundered down the court, mechanized, rehearsing a series of dribbles and passes: Sasha to Rebecca, Rebecca to Carrie, Carrie to Josie. Josie was in top form, her gold braid snapping behind her with each lunge and jump. Her breasts quivered under her jersey and spandex sports bra, and each time she landed—each time the ball connected with her hands, rattling her—Theo felt his chest tighten. If he and Mia ever had another child—as if they'd want another child together—there was a twenty-five percent chance that it would have CF like Sissy. *Chance, chances.* A gamble. Josie was a gamble, too, or maybe just a stupid risk, but she was carrying their child, and Theo felt—no, he *knew*—that their baby wouldn't be sick. Their baby would be okay.

Josie caught the ball and Lisa slid into her, knocking them both out of bounds. Theo ran over, and Josie quickly jumped to a stand. "I'm okay," she said. She still had the ball.

"I think you should take a break," he told her. The gym was suddenly very quiet.

"I'm fine," she said, tapping a nervous rhythm on the orange skin. She started to dribble and put a hand out to block Lisa. "Come on, babe. Let's do this."

Theo leaned forward and knocked the ball out of the way, mid-bounce. "I told you to take a break," he said. The ball rolled across the floor, and he imagined that every eye in the gym was following its path. "So take one, unless you'd rather be running laps."

Josie stared at him, face bright with sweat, then bounced on her toes. "All right," she said. She started to jog, and the rest of the girls looked at each other, then at Theo, and he knew he had to go on with practice or lose them all completely. He clapped his hands two times. "Back to the court," he said. He pointed to Amanda, who was on the bench. "Take her spot."

The girls resumed their drill, and Josie ran laps. Theo lifted his eyes every time she rounded the corner and passed in front of him, and her speed actually seemed to be increasing instead of slowing. Her braid trailed behind her.

"Pace yourself, Jo," Theo yelled.

She didn't look at him.

They started a new drill, and while he tried to focus as the players ran lay-ups, he watched for Josie in the periphery of his vision, sure that she would lose steam and stop at any moment. But she kept going. Thirty minutes passed this way, and though the practice shouldn't have been over yet—they had a big home game coming up against Franklin-Simpson—he called it to a halt. The girls, who normally would've been happy to have a long evening ahead of them, hovered mid-court, looking at him. "Hit the showers," he told them.

"I'd like to get a little more time in, Coach," Carrie said. "I don't feel ready for Saturday yet."

"Practice at home," he said, and pointed to the locker room. "Go on, now."

The girls jogged off court, and Josie continued to run. Her face was dripping, her hair dark now with sweat, and her pace was finally beginning to flag. Her big leg muscles trembled with every jolt against the polished wood floors.

"Stop now," Theo yelled to her. "Practice is over."

She shook her head.

"Do it, goddammit!" he said. "Unless you want to ride the bench Saturday."

That did it, as he knew it would. She lunged off a final three or four steps, then hunched over, grasping her knees. She coughed, the sound seeming to rise from the bottom of her stomach, scraping her insides raw. Theo ran over and put a hand on her neck.

"Get the fuck off me," she gasped, knocking his hand away. Her freckled face was scarlet across the nose and cheeks, her forehead and chin still ivory. Her neck was red-streaked, too, welts that could have been made by a claw.

"You happy now?" Theo asked. He could hear a couple of the girls sneak out of the locker room behind him, could feel their eyes on his back and on Josie, who had since laid on her side and was pulling her knees to her chest. "You're going to kill that baby," he said, keeping his voice low and steady, more steady than he felt. "You're going to bleed him out right here on this gym floor you love so much, if you aren't careful."

"Good." Her eyes darted to his and away, childlike.

"You stupid bitch," he said, thinking, absurdly, of Joe. He hadn't wanted a dog—hadn't seen the sense in committing to another responsibility—but Mia had insisted, and he'd gone along. And the dog was all right. Not man's best friend, exactly, but good enough. Joe didn't get walked much, but when the walking got done, he was always full-steam-ahead, too. Didn't matter where they were going, or coming, he wanted to dig into the ground with his toenails and drag, *mush,* himself forward. Joe didn't care about the destination, so long as he was moving. "Maybe you don't know what's good for you," he told Josie.

She looked up at him, her cooling face now bleached, the freckles like tiny bullet holes in her fair skin. "What do you mean?"

"Have you made an appointment yet?" he whispered.

She stood up and brushed off her shorts. "I was going to tell you after practice."

"Come to my office," he said, leading them off the court.

He could still hear showers running in the locker room as they walked to his office, so he closed and locked the door behind them, hoping anyone remaining would assume he and Josie had both gone home. Unlikely, given the public nature of their weird argument, but he couldn't think about that right now. "What did you find out?" he asked her.

"It'll be four hundred," she said.

He nodded, relieved but detached. This wasn't as bad as it could be.

"I found out about this clinic in Louisville online," Josie said. "So I called them, and they told me I'd have to come in for counseling, then wait twenty-four hours, because of some law.

The closest day I could get was next Friday for the counseling, then Saturday for the other."

"Saturday's the Todd County game," Theo said.

"We'll just have to miss it."

He rubbed his forehead and laughed. "You can miss it, maybe. But I can't, hon. What would people think, both of us gone? It wouldn't look right."

She was very still. "It would look a lot worse if I started to show."

She was right, of course. But part of him was picturing his future, *their* future, and how quickly a thing like this—her one remaining semester of high school, the fifteen years between them—would blow over in this town. People would probably be more upset if they found out about Mathias's little stash in the Head Coach's lounge, the nicer office near the boys' locker room, with the windows. People in this town would understand that there's a difference between taking drugs, being purposefully incompetent, and falling in love with the wrong person. Because he *did* love Josie, he was sure of it. He wanted to do right by her, and he wanted to hold on to her. People here would understand that, too. And if they didn't, so what? There was always Bowling Green or Lexington or somewhere else.

"No, it wouldn't look right at all," he said, mostly to himself.

Her face crumpled—that was the only word for it—but she still didn't understand him, still didn't realize what he was proposing. She drew an invisible line on his desk with her finger, trembling, and then the action turned loopy, and her face drew into her old sexy look that Theo knew so well, and he was fascinated by how he could follow her thought process with that one nervous finger, like she was a planchette, divining messages from a supernatural power.

"We could make a whole weekend out of it," she said. "We could go early, you know? Maybe go to Kentucky Kingdom—"

"They'll be closed," Theo said. "For winter."

"Aw, that doesn't matter. Not there, then. We'll have dinner somewhere nice. And I can wear something for you. Real special."

"What would you wear?" Theo asked. He sensed his cruelty, but he was also following her, imagining with her. Honeymoon: the word seemed silly, ridiculous, even, but he thought it anyway.

She tilted her head. "You know," she said, blushing, "like a nightie or something. The night before won't matter. We can really live, right? It'll be the best time."

"And that sounds like living to you," Theo said. "Dinner and a movie and then we get this baby taken care of. Might as well make a big weekend out of it, right? You want to tour the Slugger museum while we're there?"

She stopped tracing with her finger. "You're screwing with me, aren't you?"

"No way," he said.

"You're not going to take care of this."

"I'm going to take care of you," he told her. "I just don't know that this is the way to do it."

She started to cry, the first time he had ever seen her do it. "You bastard. You selfish asshole. I'll tell. I'll tell the principal."

"Tell her," Theo said. She wouldn't, he felt sure. She had as much at stake as he did. He thought about Sissy, his insurance.

I don't care, he told himself. *None of that has to matter anymore*. There were other schools, other jobs—positions at factories, right in this very county, that paid better than teaching did. He saw it all suddenly: an apartment like the kind he'd had in college—a house was too much, why had he and Mia been so dead set on mortgaging one?—Josie on the bed beside him, Sissy on the weekends. He could be a better father to his child on the weekends. And she'd have a brother or sister to play with and love, maybe a boy who could help look out for her. Was it wrong for him to imagine this life? Was he crazy for thinking that he could save himself by saving this baby?

Josie picked his cup of pencils up off his desk and threw it against the wall, but the sound was small, lightweight, and Theo could tell that the gesture embarrassed her. "I'll tell my mom!" she yelled.

"Calm down," he said, waving his hands at her, open palms patting air.

"My scholarship," she whispered.

"Honey," he said, "you can still use it. We could do this."

She ran out of his office. He didn't follow her, but he felt certain she would come around. He wasn't being reasonable, exactly, but this was the right thing to do. His adrenaline was high—he hadn't felt this way since college, when his own feet pounded the court, matching his heartbeat.

When he came home from that night's practice, Mia was in the kitchen, scrubbing the counters, and Sissy was in her bassinet across the room. Much as he'd been disgusted by the state of the house for the last several months—and the dog, the dog had been the most senseless, irresponsible kind of loss—it hurt him to see his wife like this: so ardently domestic, so desperately sorry. She raised a finger to her lips when he walked into the kitchen, and he wondered if he was supposed to play a part in this sweet little moment: tip-toe across the linoleum in his sneakers, silently plant a kiss on her forehead, then her mouth. She had an apron on, for Christ's sake; should he untie the neat bow, unbutton her clean blouse? He remembered her as she'd been before the burden of Sissy's birth and disease had landed so heavily on them both: not his soulmate, maybe, but a woman to feel proud of. A woman to feel good about coming home to. Mathias had called her "eleven different kinds of fine" just after Theo came to Rome High School, and that was maybe the best compliment he'd ever been paid. She'd been dark-haired and lively and lovely. She'd been a thing worth beholding.

Her eyes now, though, were just as empty to him as they'd been the night Joe died. She smiled and turned back to the counter, yellow rubber gloves brushing the bends of her elbows as she scrubbed hard water stains out of the grooves around the faucet, SOS pad rasping against the stainless steel. Maddeningly single-minded. He went to the bassinet, leaned over his daughter, and brushed his lips against the satiny skin of her temple. She was gorgeous, tiny, doll-like. Mia took good care of her. Theo worried for them both—and already, the thrill of deciding to be with Josie and raising their child was ebbing, becoming entangled and complex. Sissy sighed in her sleep: a luxurious sound that made Theo ache. He wished he could have done better by her. He'd spent the first few months of her life resenting her, despite himself; he'd expected hard work and lost sleep, but he hadn't been prepared for the sudden changes in Mia, who cried so often that her face always shined and who told Theo one night, with a calm that chilled him, that she was thinking about swallowing a bottle of pills. He understood that what he and Mia had was fine in the good times, when they could rent movies and eat out and shop for a new car together. Hard times were another matter. Then Sissy started getting sick, and he realized at some point that he wasn't thinking of her as a child anymore, or as his daughter: she was a hypothetical, a baby who may or may not live to see thirty, and if he expected too much, or loved her too much, he'd be disappointed. Her weakness dismayed him, but he was weaker. "Night, baby," he whispered, and Sissy sighed again. He went straight to bed.

Mia slipped in beside him an hour later, skin still faintly redolent of Windex and Lysol. "I do the best I can," she whispered against his back, and the sensation stirred him, surprised him. She ran her fingers lightly across his ribs, tickling.

"I know you do," Theo said. He rolled over and kissed her, slipped his hand into the open neck of her gown, touching the familiar slope of her breast—the first time in a long time, and maybe, he thought, the last. He traced the line of her collarbone, making a chart in his head, two-columned: *Mia, Josie*. One bigger in the chest, one taller. One with lines at the corner of her eyes, one with acne clustered around her temples. He thought about songs they liked—songs he thought they liked—and the way they wanted to be touched. One of them liked him to flick his tongue lightly across the nape of her neck, where her real hair turned into the fuzzy, baby-down of soft skin. One liked him to breathe into the cup of her ear, not words, just heat.

He couldn't remember which was which right now. Sissy slept, and as he pushed the gown up around his wife's hips, raking his boxers down at the same time with his knees and then his feet, he imagined the wet gurgle of her chest as she drew in air, mobile of stars suspended above her, the moon a smiling crescent in neon.

They won the game against Franklin-Simpson. He and Josie had never been so in synch. It seemed like he merely had to *think* an instruction and Josie reacted: cut quickly to the left, passed the ball to Lisa, who was open, took the chance at the three-pointer and made it, sealing the victory. At some point in the game, he looked up at the bleachers, and in a throng of black and gold sweatshirts and flags, he thought he saw Mia. She used to come to his games, unannounced, before Sissy was born, when she was still teaching special ed at Stevenson. She'd sit closer down, though, just behind his row of benched players. He often thought that some of the best moments in their marriage had happened then, unspoken, when the Panthers would score, the crowd would erupt, and the band would kick into "Land of a Thousand Dances," all the sounds punctuated by the occasional slide-whoop of one of those noisemakers the Band Boosters were always selling in the lobby. Amid all of this—his favorite kind of chaos—he'd turn around, savoring his moment, and see Mia just a few paces away; they'd smile at each other, and he'd know that she understood him. That she was feeling the same way he was.

This woman he thought was Mia, though, was up pretty high, just short of the second tier of bleachers that only got full at the boys' games, and she didn't smile or wave when she saw him, and why would Mia be at the game anyway? She'd no sooner bring Sissy than she'd don sequins and dance to "Tricky" with the cheerleaders at halftime. He turned away from the woman in time to see the other team score, and when he looked back, she wasn't there anymore. A guilt hallucination, he was sure. He wasn't made of stone, after all.

The game ended, and Theo felt someone sidle up beside him, shoulder hitting his shoulder.

"Theo, man," Mathias said.

Theo glanced at him, then back at the court. The girls were filing out, and Josie was already gone. He scanned the crowd for her.

Mathias stuck his hand out and Theo shook it, hesitantly. Mathias wasn't in the habit of coming to girls' games, even when his boys played the occasional Friday night game and the schedules didn't conflict. Theo had always been sore about that, but now he wanted Mathias to leave—to high-tail it back to his bachelor's pad and his dope and his easy life.

"Good game," Mathias said.

"Yeah." Theo looked over his shoulder, where the Mia look-alike had been. "Yeah, the girls did good."

Mathias crossed his arms. He was almost a foot taller than Theo, broad through the chest, and he had a presence—as a player so many years back, now as a coach—that Theo deeply envied: the reason, he knew, that Mathias was coaching boys, though they'd joked a few times together that the boys' team didn't have Josie-style perks. Uncomfortable joking.

"You're out, friend," Mathias said. He didn't lower his voice at all, but parents and teenagers were a churning mass around them, and the words felt muted, unreal. But Theo understood them.

"Out," Mathias repeated. Then he looked at the court. "I guess things got around. You know—some parent, then a teacher got involved. Then Rita Beasley."

"Well don't draw it out, for Christ's sake," Theo said. "What's going on?"

"They're having an emergency school board meeting tonight, and I expect that you'll get a call by tomorrow. That's what Noel Price told me." He sighed, and Theo could smell Listerine. "They'll let you resign. They won't want a big stir."

Sissy. Theo couldn't breathe.

"You okay?" Mathias said.

Theo laughed out loud. "She's pregnant, Matt."

"Mia?"

Theo shook his head.

"Goddamn," Mathias said.

"She's going to leave me," Theo said—out loud, but to himself. Saying it, he realized that she probably already had: *Things got around.* Mia had been in the bleachers, watching him, and now she was gone: to her mother's, with Sissy. He would come home tonight to an empty house, to the lingering smells of Joe's sickness and Sissy's baby lotion, and the rest of his life would begin. He didn't know what kind of life that could be.

"I'm sorry," Mathias told him.

Theo went to the locker room, where the girls were gathered for his wrap-up talk—Josie, nowhere to be seen—and he said the nonsense things he always said—"Good game, good teamwork, let's focus on defense at practice this week"— watching the girls' faces, wondering who among them knew.

All of them, of course, but they made their expressions innocent and blank, and he appreciated them for it. He said a prayer
with the girls and called it a night, and he could hear, leaving,
their talk shift from *amens* to discussions of parties—Chad's
house or Tresten's?—prom dates, and *man, we were so fucked up!*
It occurred to him that Josie had a second life, too. On game
nights, when Theo went home to Mia, changed a token diaper,
and made himself watch Sissy sleep, she was over at some kid's
house, nursing a bottle of Boone's Farm that somebody's older
brother had charged her eight bucks for. She studied for tests,
asked her mother for money. In another month or two she'd
start shopping for prom dresses, and whatever she'd find would
look awkward and hopeful, and on prom night she'd stand out
in the middle of this very gymnasium wearing too much eye-
shadow and lipstick, unsure for once, graceless.

He saw her as he was walking to his car, the February night
air like Novocain to his bare arms. She was with Jatarius in the
parking lot and the light from a security lamp fell over them
softly, the scene picturesque, staged. She was still in her jersey—
she'd never showered—and Jatarius was working his big hands
up and down her bare arms, warming them, and in a moment
Theo knew that they would kiss, that Josie was just waiting for
him to see it. He could get in his car and follow them—she'd
let him, she'd make sure Jatarius slowed down, using any excuse that came to mind; and he'd do it, do whatever she asked,
spurred on by the promise of her. He'd do it, because Josie was
a girl—a woman—who would, Theo was understanding, have
her way: with his help or without it. Now, no more than thirty
feet away, she lifted her chin, and Jatarius lowered his, and they
were a single dark shadow outlined in a hazy yellow nimbus—

gone already, she was telling him, and he was a fool to think otherwise.

Later, he could turn off on whatever country road they turned off on, drive a little past the thick of trees where they'd park, and pull his own vehicle over to the shoulder, quieting the engine, shutting off the headlights. His overcoat was in the passenger seat. He'd put it on, creep back down the road, take a spot behind the trunk of a leafless water maple. And they'd watch each other through the rear windshield of Jatarius's car: Josie's slow undress, her mount, her gentle rocking, baby between them.

HARPER PERENNIAL CELEBRATES THE SHORT STORY

CLASSIC MASTERS OF THE SHORT FORM

The Bohemian Girl
by Willa Cather
ISBN: 978-0-06-177378-5

A Disgraceful Affair
by Fyodor Dostoyevsky
ISBN: 978-0-06-177374-7

Family Happiness
by Leo Tolstoy
ISBN: 978-0-06-177373-0

An Experiment in Misery
by Stephen Crane
ISBN: 978-0-06-177377-8

The Happy Failure
by Herman Melville
ISBN: 978-0-06-177375-4

The Model Millionaire
by Oscar Wilde
ISBN: 978-0-06-177376-1

Each classic short will feature a bonus short story by a contemporary writer.